FIFTY-ONE SHADES OF GREEN

THE EMERALD INN-BEHIND CLOSED DOORS

JUDITH SESSLER

FIFTY-ONE SHADES OF GREEN

THE EMERALD INN-BEHIND CLOSED DOORS

ALL CHARACTERS PORTRAYED ARE FICTITIOUS. ANY RESEMBLANCE TO REAL PERSONS, LIVING OR DEAD, IS PURELY COINCIDENTAL

ALSO BY JUDITH SESSLER

FIFTY SHADES OF GREEN
OR
COFFEEHOUSE CONFESSIONS OF THE AVERAGE JOE
copyright 2016 by Judith Sessler

SAINTS AND SINNERS
SHORT STORIES FROM THE BIZARRE TO THE SUBLIME
copyright 2016 by Judith Sessler

THE TRAVEL KIDS SERIES

BOOK ONE
BOTHERSOME BOBBY AND THE TRAVEL KIDS
copyright 2016 by Judith Sessler
BOOK TWO
THE TRAVEL KIDS - THE RESCUE OF PRINCESS OKALANI
copyright 2017 by Judith Sessler
BOOK THREE
THE TRAVEL KIDS - CURSE OF THE PHAROAH'S TOMB
copyright 2017 by Judith Sessler

DEDICATION

To my dedicated readers who asked for more of Randy after reading ...

FIFTY SHADES OF GREEN

COFFEEHOUSE CONFESSIONS OF THE UNCOMMON JOE

ACKNOWLEDGMENTS

I wish to thank my husband for the love and support he has given me for forty-nine years, through the ups and downs, and ins and outs. We've traveled this bumpy road together and stood side by side, toe to toe and shoulder to shoulder, weathering all the storms and celebrating all the blessings.

I especially want to thank him for sharing his expertise about WWII and guiding me through my research to assure a true and realistic picture of the times.

Bill, I love you to the moon and back and 'til the end of time.

TABLE OF CONTENTS

PROLOGUE

3

A New Beginning

She missed him terribly. Jimmy had been a dear friend when he was alive and was, even more so, after his death. Jimmy changed her life and gave her a chance to finally find happiness.

He had always been there for her. At the drop of a hat, he would come and rescue her from her pathetic excuse of a car. Her eighteen year-old Camaro was held together with spit and a prayer, but Jimmy could always get her running. Time after time, out of the kindness in his heart, he saved Randy from being late for work or stranded somewhere, usually in the middle of nowhere.

Seventeen years ago, her piss-poor excuse of a husband ran off with a pregnant teenager and left her with a newborn baby and the Camaro. At first she was devastated, but as time passed she realized it was the best thing that could have ever happened to her and her son Noah. She moved in with her mother and together they raised a son she was very proud of. He was an honorable young man with impeccable integrity, the exact opposite of her no-good, low-life, worthless ex-husband. Randy heard that after he left *her*, Kevin left his girlfriend in the same position...except he never married her. One night, he just disappeared into thin air and his teenybopper girlfriend was left to raise her illegitimate child alone. Randy felt very sorry for the poor, young girl who had been fooled by Kevin's disarmingly, good looks and affable charm. Despite her mother's warnings, Randy had fallen for the same things.

So the only tangible remnant of their marriage was the wonderful son she adored and an eighteen year-old Camaro that was the bane of her existence.

Jimmy, her favorite customer at the designer coffeehouse she managed, was her savior. He never asked to be compensated. He just came to her rescue, whenever, or wherever, she needed it.

Randy was eternally grateful for his selfless kindness and it was only after his funeral that she learned how much her friendship meant to him.

At the graveside, an unknown man in a long dark coat handed her two envelopes that changed her life. When she opened the first, she sobbed.

Dear Randy,

If you are reading this, then I have gone to a better place. Please don't be sad. I had as good a life as one could expect. Life threw me some curves and some heartaches. But all in all, I was content at the end.

And that was because of you, Randy. I never told you how much you meant to me. You were always a kind and gentle person who made me feel like I wasn't alone in the world anymore.

My life was so lonely after I lost Angie and the baby, but you drew me back out of myself so I could find some peace at last.

Please don't ever forget how much you changed my life, and remember me whenever you think that you don't make a difference in the world.

God bless you, Randy

Your friend,

Jimmy

She went back to read the other letter in the envelope.

LAST WILL AND TESTAMENT OF
JAMES L. MUSGROVE

Randy stared down at the paper in disbelief. Jimmy had left her everything. He had an insurance policy of $100,000, a policy he had taken out after he met Randy. He left her his three bedroom house and his share of the repair shop he co-owned.

But the most important and precious thing he left her was something she would cherish forever — a brand new car.

Now here it was five years later, and thanks to him, her life was completely transformed.

Between the insurance money and all of Jimmy's other assets, she was able to purchase a small inn that she lovingly restored. She named it the Emerald Inn because whenever she saw him, Jimmy was wearing a bright-green baseball cap.

There were times at night, when the Inn was quiet, she felt his presence and would whisper softly, with tears in her eyes.

...thank you Jimmy...

CHAPTER ONE

Randy

The shrill tone of the alarm awakened Randy at the set time of five a.m. She had the ringer set to its quietest setting so as not to disturb any of the Inn's guests. It wasn't usually necessary to set an alarm at all because she was an early riser. Years of opening the coffeehouse at four-thirty in the morning trained her body to wake up on its own. But *this* morning she needed the extra sleep.

She took a bracing, ice-cold shower to wake up. She had been awoken at three a.m. by an inebriated guest who lost his front door key. The evening desk clerk ended his shift at eleven o'clock, so Randy covered any overnight needs the guests might have. They were usually few and far between, but she had a feeling Doug Lagerfeld was going to be the exception, and she was right. He came in, stinking drunk. She had to steer him to his room and prevent him from stumbling into the walls. Luckily, he wasn't loud or obnoxious. She unlocked the door to his room and he staggered in. He whispered his drunken, slurred words of thank you and collapsed on the bed. He was snoring before she reached the door.

It wasn't often that her guests appeared in that condition, unless it was a stag night for a wedding party or a group of businessmen letting loose, but Doug Lagerfeld was there to finalize his divorce and his, soon-to-be, ex-wife was in the next room. She didn't know any of the details and she didn't *want* to know.

As Innkeeper, Randy was a gracious hostess. She made sure her guests were afforded their privacy, if that's what they wanted, but there were other guests whose gregarious nature drew her, and other guests, into lively conversations in the parlor. Friendships were often made, lingering around the fire, drinking coffee and sharing stories. It was one of the things she loved best about owning the Inn.

Randy threw on a pair of dark-blue, denim jeans and a soft, red wool sweater. It would be chilly in the parlor until she lit the fire in the fireplace. It was a relatively small room so it heated quickly. She prided herself on the cozy, yet elegant, feel to the room.

When she bought the Inn, it needed only a few improvements. The guest rooms were already decorated in soft, elegant, pastel hues. They were furnished with beautiful four poster beds, luxurious bedding and thick, plush carpeting. Every bathroom was tiled with white and grey-swirled marble and well-appointed with upscale, bronze fixtures. Most of the bathrooms sported jacuzzi bathtubs, steam showers, and sumptuous towels made of Egyptian cotton. Thick, terrycloth robes with matching slippers were found in every closet. There was nothing that needed to be done to the guest rooms to ready them for visitors.

The parlor, on the other hand, was in dire need of some tender-loving care. It wasn't totally unsuitable, but it just wasn't Randy's style. Its furniture was dated and decorated with dark, dreary shades of burgundy and forest green. The draperies were heavy brocade that didn't allow the bright, morning sunlight to stream in through the large, glass windows.

Randy redecorated with pastel furnishings of cream and pale green. The sofas were plush and comfortable, in stark contrast to the firm, uncomfortable ones they replaced. It was understated and elegant, yet had a warm, cozy atmosphere that welcomed guests to sit and relax. The walls were decorated with paintings from different local artists. The large, wood-burning fireplace was the focal point of the room. Even in warmer weather, the guests wanted a fire lit for the ambiance.

It was her favorite room. She would make a strong cup of coffee from the coffee bar and allow herself to sit for a few moments in the solitude before guests wandered in. It provided her the time to gather her thoughts and switch into innkeeper mode.

This morning her thoughts wandered to the gratitude she felt for Jimmy's generosity which enabled her to buy the Inn. She had accidentally stumbled upon it when it was in foreclosure. It had been repossessed by the bank and was going to auction. She marveled that there was only one other interested party and her bid was the highest. The bank wanted to quickly unload the millstone that was a money-pit, so she was able to buy it at far-below market value. The day of the closing she felt as if Jimmy were watching from above.

She was startled from her reverie when Margaret Ashworth wandered in.

"Oh, excuse me, Mrs. Ashworth," Randy said as she stood up and took her coffee mug with her.

"No, no, my dear. Please, sit. I don't wish to disturb you," she said politely in her thick English accent.

"Thank you, no," Randy replied, embarrassed she was caught "sitting down on the job."

It was very early, before the crack of dawn, but Margaret Ashworth was an early riser like herself. She was a sweet, elderly British woman who was there to celebrate her 70th wedding anniversary with her husband, Edward. Randy wanted to make sure their celebration would be a memorable one. The Ashworths deserved extra-special treatment...seventy years, after all...*seventy years!*...unheard of.

Their marriage survived World War II — the blitz, the carnage, the destruction of London, and all of its aftermath...a feat that few people nowadays could truly appreciate or understand.

"Let me get your tea, Mrs. Ashworth," Randy said.

"Oh, how sweet of you, dear."

"My pleasure."

Mrs. Ashworth smiled at her gratefully.

Margaret had always been a strong, independent woman, but the years were wearing on her. Randy could tell it was difficult for her to get around, but she knew you would never hear her complain. Her English pride wouldn't permit it.

Randy took out one of her special, delicate porcelain teacups, the ones with the miniature roses on it, the ones she reserved for dignified little old ladies, and poured her a cup of Earl Grey tea. She put a thin slice of lemon on the side, just the way she knew Mrs. Ashworth liked it. Randy had a keen eye and kept track of the little things, the details that would make her guests feel like they were the only ones at the Inn. It was what made her an Innkeeper Extraordinaire.

"Would you like a blueberry scone? They're fresh out of the oven," she said as she laid the cup in front of Margaret.

"Oh that would be lovely, my dear. You are so thoughtful."

"I'll be right back."

Randy went into the kitchen, where the luscious smell of freshly baked pastries filled the air. Angie was just removing the last tray of croissants from the oven.

"Good morning Angie."

"Hey, Randy."

She insisted the staff be on a first name basis with her. She didn't want them to feel like it was just another job.

When she managed the coffeehouse, she knew that if the employees felt they weren't just a number, they would put their best foot forward and give their all. Occasionally, there would be a lazy or dishonest odd duck who had sticky fingers in the till, but Randy quickly weeded them out and gave them the boot. Her least favorite part of the job was having to fire someone. So here at the Inn...*her* Inn, she surrounded herself with employees who were more like family. And that's exactly how she treated them.

"How's Jack?" she asked.

"Oh, he's getting there. He has a doctor's appointment this morning to take the cast off."

Angie's husband tripped and broke his ankle at work and had been laid up for six weeks. She knew how much of an extra burden it was for Angie. Considering she was "family," Randy gave her the first week off, with pay, to settle Jack in.

Angie was her angel in the kitchen who worked her magic in the wee hours of the morning. While she was gone, Randy had the formidable task of providing her guests with a fairly acceptable continental breakfast. She could hard-boil eggs, put out bowls of fruit and lay out cereal and bagels. But it was the pastries...Angie's fresh-baked pastries...that would be the challenge. Whatever was she going to do?

But God bless her heart, Angie came in the night after Jack's accident to make enough pastry dough to last the week. She wrapped each of them individually and put them in the freezer. She wrote out detailed instructions. Randy might be an extraordinary innkeeper, but she couldn't even make slice and bake cookies to save her life.

"I bet Jack's happy about that," Randy said as she took a scone from the cooling rack and placed it on a plate.

"I am, too," she chuckled. "They're going to put him in a boot, so he'll be off the crutches. Not that I mind waiting on him hand and foot, pardon the pun, but it's like waiting on a six year-old. Men, such big babies," she said as she laughed.

Angie and Jack had been married for eight years and had the usual struggles. Randy wondered if *they* would be able to weather the marital storms to survive seventy years. She hated to be pessimistic, but in a world that focused on self, the odds were against the majority of marriages.

On her way back to the parlor she turned on the sound system. Soft classical music playing in the background created a tranquil mood for her guests. At the coffeehouse, music was geared more towards the trendy, younger crowd and atmospheric elevator music would never fly.

"Here you go, Mrs. Ashworth," Randy said.

She smiled as she laid the plate down in front of her.

"Oh, please. Call me Margaret."

Randy smiled back, but there was no way in hell she could ever call her by her first name. It would just feel too disrespectful.

By now several other guests were filtering in and helping themselves to breakfast. Randy greeted them all and then headed to the front desk.

"Good morning, Carly."

"Hey, Randy. How ya doin'?"

"Not too bad. Mr. Lagerfeld lost his key and came in drunk at 2am."

"I'm not surprised. They both looked pretty upset when they checked in. He told me they've been married for over twenty years."

"Do you know when they're meeting with the lawyers?"

"Mrs. Lagerfeld said it's today."

As front desk clerk, Carly knew the comings and goings of the guests. When they checked in, they usually told her the reason for their stay. Most of them would reveal things about themselves — private, sensitive things, simply because they knew they would only see her when they checked in and then again when they checked out. Somehow they felt safe sharing confidences with a total stranger they would never see again.

Carly was a treasure and so was Reuben.

They were two of the hardest working baristas at the coffeehouse. She knew Carly would make a perfect front desk clerk and she wanted Reuben as her assistant. Besides, if she hired one, she had to hire the other. The two of them came as a matched set.

Wherever Carly went, Reuben went, because

they had history...intense history.

It was a night that none of them would ever forget.

Carly and Reuben were just starting to close up the coffeehouse when a polite, good-looking man came in. Carly waited on him and was lured by his muscular build and disarmingly good looks. Reuben watched their encounter and sensed there was something ominous about him so he called the police. As it turned out, his instincts were right. The charming young man who was flirting with Carly, was a kidnapper, rapist and murderer on the run. The police, with sirens blaring and lights flashing, surrounded him before he knew what was happening and a tragedy was averted.

Reuben had saved Carly from a fate worse than death, and maybe from death itself, and she never looked at him the same way again. He had always just been the quiet, gentle, freckle-faced guy she worked side-by-side with. But now, he was her hero.

When it came to the fact that Reuben was

completely in love with her, she was blind as a bat.

He had fallen in love with her the moment they started working together, but he never dared reveal his feelings because he knew he simply wasn't in her league. She was beautiful and compelling and Reuben knew she could never fall for a skinny, red-headed geek like him.

"How does it look for tonight?" Randy asked.

"Fully booked. The Garret wedding party is arriving at four. They are in 208, 209, and 210."

"Good. Make sure there's chilled champagne in each room," she said, but knew Carly didn't need reminding.

Carly always had the rooms equipped with whatever complimentary items were appropriate, whether it was flowers, champagne, a fruit basket, or in the case of the Lagerfelds, just a welcome card and commemorative booklet on the history of the Inn. The Lagerfelds were certainly not celebrating anything they would want to remember in the future.

When Randy bid on the Inn, she knew it was located in an ideal location. There were several wedding venues in close proximity, as well as several colleges and private prep-schools.

The schools filled her up seasonally during graduations and parents weekends, and the weddings kept her busy all year long.

There was no question about it, the Inn was profitable and insured her a secure future, unlike the shaky one she had before Jimmy's gift.

As she walked back into the parlor to attend to her guests, she felt his presence, again.

and once again, she whispered,

...thank you, Jimmy...

CHAPTER TWO

Room# 201 ... *Bobbi Lagerfeld*

Bobbi woke with a pounding headache. It might have had something to do with the fact she spent the first half of the night crying her eyes out, and then couldn't fall asleep until 4 a.m. The rooms were soundproof, but if you strained your ears, you could hear the neighboring doors open and close. She waited up until she heard Doug come in. She could only hear the door close and nothing else, but she knew he had come back drunk. For the past six months, ever since she asked for the divorce, he came home in that condition, more often than not.

She groaned when she looked at the clock

and saw that it was only 5:30. She rolled over, pulled the goose down comforter over her head, and tried to go back to sleep, but she knew it was futile. The thoughts in her jumbled brain were swirling and bouncing off each other like ping pong balls in a funnel cloud.

She grumbled as she swung her legs over the side of the bed and onto the plush carpet. She slipped into the thick, terrycloth robe and slippers.

There was no one to talk to, so she had to talk to herself. She pulled the soft robe around her and thought, well, if I have to go through this nightmare, at least I can do it in comfort.

She shivered, not because the room was cold, but because memories were flooding in like a raging hurricane.

She was thinking about their honeymoon with melancholy tenderness. She remembered lying in Doug's arms and waking to the sounds of tropical birds. She remembered being wrapped in each others loving embraces, dreaming of the perfect, magical, life they were going to have together…forever.

They would rise early, make love…then make love again…the hallmark of a perfect honeymoon. Then they'd stroll, hand in hand, on the white, sandy beach outside their room. They would gaze into each other's eyes with hunger, return to their room and make love…again. They had breakfast in bed, lunch in bed, dinner in bed, with "snacks" in-between. The only time they left their room was for their walks on the beach to watch the glorious sunsets. When they returned home and friends asked what they thought of beautiful Jamaica, they just looked at each other, smiled, and said it was paradise. Then they would giggle. They had seen nothing of Jamaica.

Bobbi met Doug in grad school. He was just finishing up his Doctoral thesis in international business management and she was working on her Master's in childhood education. They were both academics with exceptional minds and plans for a brilliant future. You would think that with those prodigious qualifications on their marital resume, they would be able to solve any problems that could possibly arise.

When they graduated, Doug secured an impressive, well-paid position with an international banking firm and Bobbi went to work for a state-run, educational facility designed to reform early-childhood programs.

They were becoming well-established in their careers, with salaries befitting their rising success. They contemplated buying a condo in the city, but opted instead for an impressive, modern-architecture home in the suburbs.

Their social circle included other career-minded thirty-somethings devoted to their own chosen fields. They got together to dine on gourmet food, drink expensive wine and discuss the state of the world. Their combined intellect could probably have solved the problems of a small poverty-stricken nation.

They were 100% committed to their careers and understood each other's passion for their own profession. Bobbi planned to go back to school and earn her Doctorate. Her ultimate goal was a tenured professorship at a prestigious university.

They were perfectly suited for each other and they were living their dream.

Then the unexpected happened. Bobbi became pregnant. You would think that two exceptionally intelligent people could figure out how *not* to become pregnant. But to their dismay and regret, Bobbi didn't fall into the 99% category of birth-control pill efficacy, and with that 1% gap in effectiveness, she drew the short straw.

They were totally caught off-guard.

They had decided, even before they were married, that they didn't want children. In their world of academia, children simply didn't fit into their lifestyle and neither of them felt the need, nor the desire, to raise a child.

Both sets of their parents were horrified.

"What do you *mean* you don't want kids?" Doug's mother asked.

"How can you *not* want babies??" Bobbi's mother exclaimed incredulously.

Bobbi came from a family of seven, her parents and five children and Doug had four brothers and sisters. It was inconceivable that they wanted to remain childless. How could this be? After all, didn't they know that was one of the primary reasons to get married in the first place? Get married, have babies. As far as their parents were concerned, no discussion was necessary. Couldn't they see that with their combined intellect they would spawn exceptional children who could contribute much to society? They tried to appeal to their social conscience. All these were the arguments they presented to Doug and Bobbi, over and over again...but to no avail.

So when they announced that Bobbi was "with child," their parents were ecstatic. They looked at it as an act of fate. If their kids weren't going to make the leap towards parenthood, a higher power intervened and did it for them. They were over the moon at the prospect of becoming grandparents. Baby clothes were bought; baby showers were planned; cribs, strollers and carseats were gifted.

Bobbi and Doug remained in shock and were unable to celebrate the fact that a child was about to enter their lives. They tried to envision a future that included the one thing they didn't plan on, or heaven knows, didn't want. They knew their lives would be dramatically changed and to say they weren't happy was a gross understatement.

It was decided, right from the get-go, that Bobbi wasn't going to leave her job. She felt absolutely *no* maternal instinct and knew that wasn't going to change just because she held a newborn baby in her arms. They would employ a well-educated, well-qualified nanny who would raise their child. And that was the end of that.

For appearance sake, they tried to show a modicum of enthusiasm to the friends and family who were thrilled to death for them. Three baby showers were given and the nursery was filled to overflowing.

As Bobbi's due date approached, she had to cut back a few hours at work. She was extremely physically fit, but found she was becoming overwhelmingly tired by late-afternoon.

Then the day came when Bobbi went into labor. There was little said on their way to the hospital — no excitement for the imminent birth of their child. It was just the opposite.

They knew from the ultrasound that the baby was a boy. It was practical to know the sex of the baby ahead of time, and detached practicality was the name of the game for them.

It was a long and arduous labor and Bobbi managed well, until the very end when she succumbed to the pain.

"Okay, Bobbi, I see the baby's head. Just a few more pushes and you'll be meeting your little baby boy," the doctor said.

Doug remained at his wife's side, mopping her brow and letting her squeeze the hell out of his hand. He didn't take it personally when she called him a goddamn asshole because he was warned that women lost their minds towards the end of labor.

"Okay, Bobbi, hold up...hold up. Don't push," he said again.

The doctor signaled the nurse to his side.

His voice was calm, but she could tell by the look on his face there was something wrong and she was right.

It was called a nuchal cord...the umbilical cord wrapped around the baby's neck...and the doctor was unable to unentangle or cut it in time. Deprived of too much oxygen, the baby was delivered stillborn.

It wasn't until she heard the hushed silence and saw the expressions on the doctor and nurse's faces that Bobbi realized she didn't hear a baby cry.

"I'm so very sorry, Bobbi," the doctor said, as the nurse went to Bobbi's side and held her hand.

Very gently, he explained what went wrong and that it was a very rare occurrence. An accident of birth he called it and assured her there was nothing that could have been done to prevent it.

Doug leaned down and kissed her. Then he sat on the bed and held her.

She started to cry, then sob, then scream...

"No. No...*No!!!!!*" she wailed.

Doug held her and stroked her damp, disheveled hair. Her body shook and convulsed as her sobbing turned to hysteria.

Doug didn't know what to do. It was a

tragedy, yes. Before the baby even had a chance to take his first breath, he died. She was devastated and inconsolable. In the wave of emotions that coursed through his own mind and body, he watched his wife deteriorate before his eyes.

Doug had a scientific, practical mind and it just didn't compute that Bobbi's feelings could do a hundred and eighty degree turnaround in a nano-second.

Bobbi and Doug's parents went and cleared out the nursery, the one they decorated in pastel blue with teddybear embellishments. The nursery was their parents' gift. Bobbi and Doug hadn't seemed in any rush to set up a room for the baby themselves, so their parents stepped in to do it for them.

After the tragic loss of their son, Bobbi just lay silently in her hospital bed with tears streaming down her face. The nurses had to gently force her to get up and shower. She only picked at her meal trays. It was glaringly obvious she was grieving and deeply depressed. But who wouldn't be? It was infrequent that the nurses had to comfort a grieving mother. Most of the time, their job was a happy one.

Bobbi was put in a private room on another floor so she didn't have to see new parents gush and coo over their precious baby and be reminded that her arms were empty.

When they found out Bobbi was pregnant, they accepted it to the best of their ability. Neither of them had innate parental feelings, but their beliefs didn't permit them to consider termination. So they had to accept the fact, that like it or not, they were going to have a child. Yes, the death of the baby was a tragedy, but Doug had to admit to himself that he was secretly relieved.

Bobbi, on the other hand, had a flood of unexpected maternal feelings. She was told that once you had a baby, you'd experience a love like you'd never felt before. She thought it was pure hogwash, but it turned out to be true. Her heart swelled with love when she was about to see her baby and then was devastated when Luke was born dead.

They knew they should choose a name before the baby was born, so they chose Luke, but continued to referred to him as "the baby." It wasn't until the very end, when she was pushing, that Bobbi thought of him as Luke.

She was discharged home after two days, and instead of taking home a sweet, swaddled baby in her arms, she brought home an emptiness in her soul. There was a black hole where her heart used to be. Her spirit was wounded beyond repair. She knew she was never going to be the same and Doug didn't have a clue.

If he had any feelings of loss, he didn't acknowledge them, but buried them along with his son and went on with the business of living.

Bobbi's mother came every day, making her breakfast, lunch, and dinner, cleaning the house, doing the laundry, and desperately trying to pull her daughter back to life.

Bobbi had six weeks maternity leave, so she didn't have face the sorrow and pity of her friends while her emotions were so raw. Little by little, she came to terms with the crippling loss of her son.

She slowly returned to the world of the living, but she was only going through the motions. She saved her daily tears for the privacy of her bedroom when Doug wasn't home. He had retreated into his own world and was emotionally unavailable to comfort her.

So life went on, but their marriage had taken a hit. A big one. There became an unspoken distance between them that only widened over the years. They each buried themselves in their work and became increasingly successful in their own careers. They never again spoke of Luke, and to assure they never had another baby, Doug had a vasectomy.

They became strangers living in the same house, leading their own separate lives. What started out to be a union of great love and promise, was relegated to a sad, lonely and regrettable relationship. There was no strife between them, just an unspoken indifference. He moved out of the master bedroom on the pretext of a newly-developed insomnia, but in reality it was because he couldn't endure lying in bed every night, listening to Bobbi's muffled sobs, knowing there was nothing he could do. Finally, Doug began to spend his free time in the study and she fashioned her own living space in the master bedroom. Eventually, they cooked for themselves and ate their meals separately. They were cordial and polite to each other and there was an unspoken acceptance between them that they would never again be lovers and soulmates.

Now, twenty years later, they were in separate hotel rooms, getting ready to end their misery.

What was it that precipitated Bobbi's desire for a divorce after all those years of living in a functional, workable, yet empty relationship? What changed?

Now in her forties, Bobbi began to feel that her life wasn't over yet. It was as if a heavy, black curtain lifted and she could see daylight for the first time since Luke's death. At first, she became interested in little things, sunshine on her face, walks in the park, being awed by the beauty of nature. She had long-since forgotten those things because of the grief she felt. She lost her son, and then she lost her soulmate. She had walled herself off from the world for so long, that the baby steps she was taking seemed like an emotional marathon. But little by little, her world expanded until the day a spark ignited and set her world on fire.

Suddenly, she wanted to try everything and go everywhere. Her world literally exploded into a rainbow of colors. She took a painting class and found great satisfaction in creating something with her own hands. Her excitement was palpable. There was only one problem. Doug wasn't able to just flip a switch after all those years of isolation and come to life along with her. It was too late. His feelings were dead and buried.

She couldn't blame him. She *didn't* blame him. When Luke died, she died too. She became a shell of the person she *had* been — wife, lover, and soulmate. When she withdrew from life, she cut herself off, emotionally, from Doug. In the beginning he tried to draw her out, but she was unreachable, and eventually, for his own sanity, he stopped trying and let her go.

So now it was time to let *him* go.

She was abandoning him for a different kind of life...a life she planned on participating in.

No, it *wasn't* fair and she felt very guilty for causing him so much pain, but it was something she had to do, no matter what.

She had already waited too long.

CHAPTER THREE

Room# 202 ... *Doug Lagerfeld*

It was love at first sight. He had watched her from a distance, walking across the Quad, drinking coffee in the cafeteria, rushing off to class with her raven hair blowing in the wind. He was smitten, not just by her beauty, but by the way she giggled and laughed with her friends, by the energetic, bubbly personality and sweet nature he witnessed from afar.

Doug tried to work up the courage to introduce himself, but it turned out to be a twist of fate that brought them together.

He was walking out of the cafeteria, preoccupied with thoughts of the dissertation he was preparing, when at the same time, Bobbi came barreling out of the glass doors. They collided and books went flying. He was mortified, but she began to laugh so hysterically that he couldn't contain himself. They both laughed until tears were rolling down their faces.

"I'm so sorry," she finally said.

He could feel the heat and color rise in his face as he said, "no, no, it was my fault."

And from then on, it was like a Tom Hanks-Meg Ryan movie. They became inseparable. They ate together, studied together, laughed together... slept together. They were serious students, but Doug was far more serious than Bobbi. She would often interrupt him when he was studying to make him lighten up. No matter how hard he tried not to, he couldn't help it. Her laughter was so contagious that he would abandon whatever he was working on and join her foolishness, and eventually, they ended up in bed.

She was an exceptional lover and had a voracious appetite. With all the "interruptions," it amazed him that he was able to finish his

Doctorate on time...or at all, for that matter.

It amazed him even more, that she could refocus and switch gears so quickly and that she was able to finish *her* thesis before he finished his. They were both brilliant, but she was able to get back down to business after their lovemaking, while he still lingered in bed.

They both graduated in May and made the decision to get married the following week. Without a word to anyone, they eloped to Jamaica.

They knew there would be hell to pay when they returned, but it was their life and they intended to live it as they wanted to.

They were both offered enviable positions in their chosen professions.

Bobbi interviewed for an important job in education reform. She was very young to be hired for such a vital position, but her superior intellect and uncanny foresight landed her the job.

Equally brilliant, Doug secured an entry-level position with an impressive international banking firm and rose up quickly through the ranks. Talent was talent, after all, no matter how young you were.

They considered their life together idyllic. They worked hard at their jobs and spent all their leisure time together. When they weren't in bed, which was often, they went to art galleries and museums, the theater and the symphony. They were living the upscale, cultured lifestyle they wanted and had no desire to change it.

To their parents' consternation, they chose not to have children. Their parents weren't just disappointed, they were deeply distressed and frequently voiced their displeasure over the poor decision they felt their children had made.

Neither Doug nor Bobbi had any desire or parental instincts to bring a child into the world. It simply didn't fit into the way of life they chose for themselves, no matter *how* their parents felt.

When Bobbi missed her first period, she attributed it to the stress she felt at work from an upcoming presentation to the state education board.

Then several weeks later, she came down with a stomach bug. At least she *thought* it was a stomach bug that sent her to the bathroom to vomit in the toilet. By the time she got to work, the nausea and vomiting subsided, but it returned the next day. She may have had superior intellect, but when it came to thinking she might be pregnant, she was positively stupid. She was on the pill and took it religiously without fail, so that should have been the end of that. But it wasn't.

On the third morning, she felt bile rise up in her throat...not from morning sickness, but from fear...pure unadulterated fear.

On her way into the office, she stopped at the local pharmacy to buy a pregnancy kit. She kept telling herself that it *couldn't* be true. It *had* to be something else. They were simply too smart to let anything like that happen.

It turned out that they weren't nearly as smart as they thought. They watched the clock tick by until the fateful moment when they could look at the stick she peed on. They both gasped when they saw it had turned blue. How could such a tiny little line have the power to change their lives so drastically? ...drastically...*forever.*

They were unable to speak. Bobbi was sitting on bathroom floor and Doug was on the edge of the tub. They sat and just stared incredulously at each other.

Then Bobbi started to cry. Doug slid to the floor and put his arms around her. He was still too much in shock to say anything. Thoughts were racing through his mind at lightning speed.

Stupid, stupid, stupid, he thought. What are we going to do? Terminate? No, that really wasn't an option for them, even though this baby was very much unwanted. Could we put it up for adoption? No, idiot, that would never fly. Make the best of it? How? There simply wasn't any way to turn this into a best case scenario. Gone were their dreams of moving to New York one day and living in a glass-enclosed condo overlooking the city. Gone were the dreams of vacationing every year in romantic Tuscany, Paris or Athens. Gone were *all* their dreams.

Their parents, of course, were ecstatic. They took over all the planning for the arrival of the grandchild they thought they would never have.

It was agonizing, but Doug and Bobbi smiled and pretended they were happy.

Doug sat in his office every day and tried to find an upside to the situation. His coworkers would stop in and slap him on the back.

"Good going, buddy!"

"Congrats!"

"When's Bobbi due?"

"Is it a boy or girl?"

He tried to muster up feelings of remorse that he didn't want to be a father, but he just couldn't bring himself to feel guilty. And he knew Bobbi felt the same way.

Were they monsters? Were they selfish and self-centered? Maybe so, but a leopard can't change it's spots.

As the due date approached, Bobbi's belly swelled and her ankles looked like tree trunks. He didn't care. She had always been beautiful to him and she still was. He tried envisioning her holding a baby in a madonna-like pose but he couldn't conjure up the picture. Maybe he *was* a monster, after all. How could you shun the thought of a helpless little creature who, through no fault of its own, would be thrust into your life? Anyone else would have been thrilled. Anyone else would welcome the precious gift of a baby. Anyone else would look at it as a gift from God...a miracle of creation.

Good god, he really *was* a monster.

Then when the fateful day came and he watched his wife endure the pains of labor, his only thoughts were of her. He wasn't thinking of their son. They named him Luke, for no particular reason at all, but he never referred to him or thought of him as anything other than "the baby."

Then the unthinkable happened. Luke was born lifeless, blue...dead. It was surreal. There was a hushed stillness in the delivery room until Bobbi started to cry, then sob, then scream. She was inconsolable. His only concern was for the wife he loved above all measure. He felt nothing for "the baby."

He knew it was shock and postpartum depression that overtook her after the delivery. He tried to comfort her, but to no avail. It didn't compute that she felt such an overwhelming sense of loss. Yes, she carried the baby for nine months and felt him move and kick, but it was, after all, an unwanted baby.

Doug felt no such loss. He felt guilty that he couldn't bring himself to grieve or mourn, that he had to pretend, for Bobbi's sake.

When he brought Bobbi home, he did everything he could think of to ease her pain, but nothing he did consoled her. He became painfully aware he couldn't help bring her out of it, so he decided it was best to leave Bobbi's emotional needs to someone who was far better able to handle it. Her mother.

With a heavy heart, he threw himself back into work. Every night when he came home, she would be lying on the couch just staring out the window. He was at a loss as to what to say to her. He would just sit by her side and stroke her hair. He would wipe away the silent tears that rolled down her cheeks. As the weeks dragged by, she slowly returned to him, but it wasn't the same Bobbi who captured his heart from day one. She had changed.

Something in her was broken...very, very broken. It was her spirit. He tried to convince her to seek help...therapy, a grief support group, anything that would ease her pain and bring her back to him. He, too, was grieving, but not for Luke. He grieved for the loss of his wife...the love of his life...the only woman he would ever love.

Little by little, Bobbi slipped away from him. She returned to work and from the outside you couldn't tell that she lived with unspeakable heartbreak, one from which she would never fully recover. He gave her space so she could cope in her own way, but that was the biggest and most regrettable mistake he ever made. The space he gave her widened into an unbreachable gap that eventually heralded the end of the relationship he cherished.

Now suddenly, and without warning, she changed. She came to life. It was if she had awoken from a twenty-year coma. He watched as she came out of her shell and enthusiastically rejoined the human race.

As hard as he tried, he simply couldn't

awaken the same feelings in himself. He had been beaten down by years of heartbreak, misery and despair. He had long-since given up any hope of rekindling the lost love between them.

Doug wasn't entirely surprised when she asked for a divorce. She certainly had the grounds to sue for incompatibility. They *had* become incompatible. He desperately wished it could be different, because the love he had for her was deeply embedded in his soul and would remain there forever. There would be no other woman in his life. He would end up living alone and dying alone — a sad, lonely life.

What Bobbi never knew was, that after years of soul-searching, Doug came to realize that he was just as devastated as she was at the death of their son. He never permitted himself to allow for the possibility that in some small, dark corner of his being, he really *did* want Luke. He buried his feelings to protect his own sanity. He came to find out that the guilt he felt wasn't because he *didn't* want Luke, it was because he *did,* but denied those feelings to both himself and Bobbi. If he had admitted that he was shattered with the loss of their baby, he could have grieved along with her. They could have cried and mourned together.

Maybe, he wouldn't be sitting in a hotel room, alone and recovering from a dreadful hangover.

Maybe, he wouldn't be waiting to meet with their lawyers to sign the divorce papers that would dissolve their marriage.

Maybe, he wouldn't have to watch the woman he loved so desperately, walk out of his life.

And yet maybe, just maybe...it wasn't too late.

CHAPTER FOUR

Randy

After the morning guests had filtered in and out of the breakfast area and the dishes were cleared, the parlor became a peaceful oasis again. Randy was always tempted to sit and have one more quiet cup of coffee before getting into the business of the day. Before she bought the Inn, she envisioned the Innkeeper's job in more of a social realm.

In her mind's eye, she was going to spend the day socializing with her guests and making sure they felt at home. She thought she was going to flit about like a social butterfly.

Nothing could have been farther from

the truth. Her days started at four or five a.m., depending on number of guests registered. She had to make sure everything was set and ready to go for the day. Her social flitting about was limited to the morning breakfast time from seven to nine-thirty. She had to have a multi-tasking, eagle-eye, looking to see if the breakfast bar needed replenishing, or if a guest had forgotten to bring silverware or napkins to their table, or needed their coffee refilled. She was a cordial, hospitable hostess that tended to their every need, sometimes before they even knew they needed it. She had an uncanny, anticipatory perception and that was the reason people kept coming back. She received nothing but glowing, five-star reviews and often had to decline guests because she was fully booked.

When she purchased the Inn, she wasn't sure she'd be able to fill twenty rooms on a regular basis. She wasn't sure it would be a profitable investment at all, but she needn't have worried.

So with breakfast over, she jumped into the rest of her daily routine.

First, she would go over the details of that

night's bookings. She would read through the online reservations to see if there were any special requests...did they want a room near the lobby? Did they want the first floor or second? Did they want to order something special to be in the room, maybe a dozen roses, a box of Godiva chocolates, a bottle of Dom Perignon, etc...?

Next she would settle down to the painstakingly tedious job of bookkeeping. She was adept and fastidious with the financial affairs of the Inn, but she hated it. She brought with her a good working knowledge of basic business finances from managing the coffeehouse, but running an Inn was a horse of a different color.

Before the sale even went through, she enrolled in a crash course in accounting. She had a sharp mind and caught on quickly. By the time the Inn was in her hands, she was more than proficient with the skills she needed to assure it was a financial success. Still, she hated the job. She would much rather have spent her time in the Inn's front end business. Eventually, she planned on training Reuben to assist with some of the record keeping. She knew he would be eager and capable.

She was sitting at the computer immersed in the accounts, when there was a knock on the door. She looked up and smiled.

"Good morning, Bea," she said.

Bea was the Inn's housekeeping manager.

"Randy, you just won't *believe* it. Room 110 is trashed. There's beer bottles *everywhere*...they pulled all the linens off the beds and threw them in the bathtub and then turned on the water...there's cigarette butts everywhere...there's..." she rambled on.

"Calm down, Bea," Randy said.

She had to restrain herself from laughing. Bea was a competent, yet overly excitable, woman who took her job very personally, as if the Inn was her very own.

"It's okay. That's why we keep their credit card on file. We'll charge him for the fumigation and any other damages there are. Make a list of anything that needs replacing."

There was a strict "no smoking" policy in the rooms and it was clearly stated on their receipt that if there *was* any smoking, they would be charged a $150 fumigation fee.

Bea shook her head in disgust that someone had desecrated one of *her* rooms. She already had her two maids working on deconstructing the mess.

The occupants of Room 110 were two young gentlemen who were in town to attend a one day seminar. Carly had warned her after they checked in that they might be a bit rambunctious. Randy knew she'd have to keep a close eye on them, in case they became rowdy and disturbed the other guests.

It turned out that the only disturbance was wrecking the room. It didn't happen often that guests would act in a manner unbefitting an upscale Inn, but it did happen. And Randy would make sure she discouraged them from staying there again. She would hit them where it hurt...in the pocketbook.

It was Bea's inborn nature to be nervous and excitable. She was raised the youngest of eight children in a house filled with chaos. It wasn't bad chaos, but it was chaos just the same. Her parents were both teachers and encouraged their children to be free-spirited. Bea often wondered, by what freak of nature was she born into this family? She grew up in an environment of easy-going, boisterous, and uninhibited pandemonium. Her friends loved to come stay at her house because of the unrestrained fun they could have. Bea, on the other hand, hated it. She had a quiet nature and was overwhelmed by the daily mayhem that she had to endure. If she had her own bedroom, she could have retreated into some solitude, but with seven siblings she had to share a room with two of her sisters. Mary and Maggie were several years older than her, and unlike Bea, they both fit nicely into their family dynamics.

Bea was the odd duck in what she considered a family of squirrels, so she grew up to be nervous and unsettled. She could be skittish and excitable in situations that were unsettling to her. After she left home for college, she drove her roommates crazy with her fastidiousness. Her half of the dorm room was as neat and tidy as a hospital room and just as stark. To say she was the original minimalist was to put it mildly. Every one of her roommates requested someone else that was less neurotic to room with, so eventually the college gave her a single room of her own. Bea thought she died and went to heaven. She had peace, quiet and the ultimate...solitude. She felt like a pig in shit, but of course there would never be anything remotely resembling shit in her world.

After college, Bea continued to live the life of that quiet, orderly solitude. She had been so affected by the disorder of her childhood that she never craved the companionship of friends or the opposite sex. She was a loner, and content to be so. Her parents certainly couldn't understand her, but they never had. Her siblings had all gone on to continue the family tradition of large, free-spirited families. Their family get-togethers were pure torture for Bea, but she self-limited them to only the obligatory family functions. They all knew, and accepted, that she would stay for a minimally reasonable time and then get the hell out.

Bea graduated at the top of her class with

a degree in business management. She went to work for two years as a managerial assistant and found the environment of an office intolerable. As smart as she was, it never occurred to her she would actually have to interact with real people and how much she would hate it.

So at the ripe old age of twenty-seven, she found the perfect job — the comfortable niche of head-housekeeper in the quiet, tranquil Emerald Inn. She found tremendous satisfaction in taking a messy, disheveled room and transforming it into an immaculate, perfectly well-ordered guest haven.

Randy knew by her resume that she was far too over-qualified for the job. She suspected, that with Bea's quirky nature, there was more to her than met the eye. Randy had an uncanny nature to ferret out the best, and worst, in people and she knew that over time she would gain Bea's trust enough to discover what it was that made her bury herself away from the real world.

All she knew for now was, Bea was the perfect woman for the job.

CHAPTER FIVE

Room# 207 ... *Alec and Lorelei*

Her overnight bag was packed with the only things she would need for the night...a plunging, black-lace negligee with a matching thong, high-heeled black-satin slippers that made her legs look like they went on forever, and some other paraphernalia to ensure a night of exceptional sex.

When she went shopping for her "evening attire," she was dreaming about the romantic, sexy evening they were going to spend together. It had been quite a while since they had a chance to get away and she was anxious with anticipation. When she was driving home from the lingerie boutique, she was so engrossed with her thoughts that she nearly hit the car in front of her at the stoplight.

Oops, sorry, she said to herself.

Her face colored slightly as she felt the heat rise in her cheeks. She closed her eyes for just a second as she imagined Alec running his hand down her...

Honk, honk!

Oops, sorry, she said, again, as she looked in the rearview mirror at the annoyed old man in the car behind her.

I'd better get home and pack before I get myself, or somebody else, killed. That would certainly screw up our plans for the night and I can't let that happen. We've been planning this for far too long to let *anything* get in the way.

Lorelei luxuriated in a hot, steamy shower, thinking of the evening ahead. They would start out with a romantic dinner at their favorite French restaurant, drinking champagne and ending with her favorite, bananas flambé. After dinner, they would return to the room. The lights would be dimmed and romantic music would be playing in the background. The room would be filled with the gentle hint of vanilla musk from the candles he would light before they left for dinner. He knew that was her favorite scent. He was the most attentive, considerate, and sexy man she had ever known.

He surprised her with this getaway to celebrate the one year anniversary of the day they met. She knew how busy it was for him at the office lately and didn't think he'd remember, what most men would consider a trivial thing, much less plan to celebrate it.

Truth be told, she had almost forgotten it herself.

She toweled off and smoothed on Alec's favorite, peach-scented body lotion. He loved it when she let her thick, blonde hair air-dry into a mass of soft, luxurious curls. He would kiss her tenderly and run his hands through it. Her passion would be aroused at even the slightest touch of his hands, but when he stroked her hair, it would send a shudder through her entire body.

She was slightly disappointed when he called to say he would be a few hours late for check-in and instead of picking her up, she should meet him at the Inn. It meant they would miss a whole hour or two of their precious time together, but she didn't let him hear it in her voice. After all, he had rearranged his incredibly busy week to take the time to be alone with her. With all the effort he put into it, she could hardly complain about a few hours.

She finished packing her overnight bag and stood in front of her closet trying to decide what to wear. She had narrowed it down to two outfits...her dark-washed skinny jeans with a white, cashmere, v-necked sweater, or her sexy, red satin blouse and black pencil skirt. But then when she thought about it, it didn't really matter, because by the time he arrived, she would have already checked in and be in the room. And by that time she would be waiting for him...in bed. Their dinner reservations weren't until eight, so there would be plenty of time to begin "celebrating."

She decided on the skinny jeans since she knew they accentuated her butt. He could never resist fondling her firm, curved fanny. He wouldn't see her in them until they were getting ready to leave in the morning and she would welcome the caress before they left.

"Welcome back, Mrs. Sanders. You're in room# 207," Carly said as she smiled and handed her the keycard.

"Thank you," she said and smiled back.

Lorelei wasn't just smiling. She was beaming.

Carly thought, what a perfect couple the Sanders were. They had been there several times before and she remembered they usually ordered room service and hardly ever left their room.

Carly was jealous and hoped someday *she* would have a love like that.

"Do you need help with your bags?" she asked, but already knew the answer.

Mrs. Sanders had only one small bag with her, and Carly suspected that it, more than likely, contained only the few things she would need for their stay.

Lorelei blushed. She knew Carly wasn't

stupid and probably figured out what was in it.

"Uh, no, thanks. I've got it," she answered and giggled nervously.

Enviously, Carly watched her walk down the hallway. She was strikingly beautiful, with her tall, slim, but curvy body, thick blond hair that cascaded past her shoulders, and long, shapely legs. Lucky man, Mr. Sanders, she thought. Carly had no idea that she was just as beautiful as Mrs. Sanders, especially to Reuben.

Lorelei anxiously swiped the keycard and opened the door. She gasped when she entered the room. It was filled with dozens of her favorite, white roses, a balloon bouquet, a silver ice bucket chilling their favorite pink champagne, and a gold box of chocolate-covered strawberries on the nightstand. The bed was strewn with red rose petals and in the middle was a small silver tray. On the tray was a small box wrapped in red foil paper with a white bow. Next to the tray was a note written in Alec's handwriting. It simply said...open me...

She burst into tears. He was the most wonderful man in the world and loved to spoil her.

She sat down on the bed and unwrapped the box. It contained a beautiful pair of delicate gold-filigree earrings with tiny pearls and emeralds, so she would remember the day they met and the night they would spend together at the Emerald Inn…as if she *could* ever forget.

Alec would never forget the day they met, either. She was standing on line in front of him, waiting to order her coffee. He could smell the gentle scent of vanilla. It reminded him of the warm, sugar cookies his mother used to make. He had inadvertently moved closer to her, drawn in by her scent and the softness of the hair he wanted to reach out and touch.

He was so close, that when she turned around, she bumped into him and dropped her coffee on the floor.

"Oh, my God!" she yelled angrily as she bent down to pick up the empty, wet cup.

"I'm so *sorry*," he said as he grabbed the

rag the barista handed him before he came around the counter with a mop.

Alec bent down to help her, completely embarrassed.

She was grumbling to herself, but then was rendered speechless when she looked up into the bluest eyes she'd ever seen. Now it was *her* turn to be embarrassed, as her face turned beet red.

"No…no…it's fine…it was…it was…my fault, I'm sure," she said as he helped her to her feet.

The barista was attempting to mop up the mess, but neither Alec nor Lorelei were moving out of his way.

"Excuse me," he said politely.

"Oh, I'm sorry," they both said at the same time and started to laugh.

"Did you get burned?" he asked, with concern in his voice.

"No, I'm fine thank you," she said shyly.

They sat down at a table and the barista brought her a replacement coffee.

They started with small talk, but after

two hours, they knew everything there was about each other. Or almost everything.

It started out with them meeting for coffee. Then it graduated to dinner, and eventually, it ended up back in her apartment. She was so beautiful, with a warm, supple body that fit perfectly with his. They would lie together for hours after they made love, just holding and caressing each other. He was enamored by her sweetness and innocence. He was shocked to discover he was her first lover. How could someone so beautiful still be a virgin? She had to have been pursued by many men. He once asked her why she had waited.

"I wanted it to be special."

Her face colored with embarrassment.

"I'm glad it was me," he said as he stroked her silken hair.

She was very understanding when he explained that his business took him out of town frequently, often on weekends. Even though they only saw each other a few nights a week, they made those nights count, and it was always worth the wait.

Alec knew the things Lorelei liked, both in and out of bed. He paid attention to every little detail. He knew what her favorite color was, her favorite song, her favorite restaurant, her favorite movie, her favorite perfume. He knew pretty much everything there was to know about her.

He was so much in love with her that he was being ripped in two. How could he tell her that she was the love of his life and make her understand that he was also married and had been for eight years? How could he possibly explain that he had two children he adored and would never leave? How could he possibly explain it all to her? He knew he couldn't. At least, not just yet.

Alec met his wife when he went to work at Anderson Industries as a research analyst. Ashley was in human resources and his first contact when he started work. She gave him all the information regarding his benefits, policies and procedures, and the company disclosures to sign.

She was pleasant and pretty in an outdoorsy kind of way. She had an athletic body and spent much of her leisure time mountain climbing, cycling and such. Alec enjoyed engaging in sports, but wasn't quite the enthusiast she was.

After a few dates, they became comfortable with each other and started sleeping together. It was enjoyable, but not passionate. They became a "couple" and it was generally accepted by their friends that they would marry. And they did.

They followed the customary path — a wedding, a honeymoon, a house in the suburbs and kids. It was a cliche kind of life and perfectly acceptable to him…until he met Lorelei and was knocked for a loop.

Right from the get-go, Alec knew it was wrong, but he just couldn't stop himself. He knew it was deceitful and he knew it was cruel. He knew it was selfish, but he wanted her so desperately. He had to have her and he knew he couldn't give her up. He also knew that someday he would have to tell her the truth, and when that someday came, he knew he would. It just wasn't going to be today.

It was the anniversary of their first meeting. In his eight years with Ashley, he had never gone to such lengths to celebrate *anything*, because there had never been the depth of feeling between them that warranted it.

He personally contacted Randy to make the elaborate preparations for the room. She assured him everything would be perfect and he knew it would be. He lied to Lorelei when he said he would be held up at work. He wanted her to walk into the room and be overwhelmed with the fairytale setting.

He bought her the earrings knowing she would adore them. They were just her style. He would have loved for it to be an engagement ring, but he knew that could never happen. With deep sadness and remorse, he knew she would be shattered when he had to end it...when she found out that he was a liar and a cheat and betrayed both his wife and her. He was despicable and he knew it. He was just too much in love with her to do anything about it.

The only way he was able to pull it all off

was because his wife was so self-absorbed with the kids and her own lifestyle that she was clueless when it came to his comings and goings. It was the perfect arrangement for a man bent towards infidelity, and if that's all it was with Lorelei, he wouldn't feel guilty. But it was ever so much more.

He told Ashley he was going to be out of town for the night to attend a business seminar. Alec knew that she would never think twice to check up on him, or maybe she would and just wouldn't care.

As Alec drove towards the Inn that was fifty miles out of town, his level of excitement began to rise. He could almost taste the sweetness of her lips when they kissed. The thought of caressing her milky-white skin and feeling her body pressed against his was almost more than he could bear. He hungered for her more than words could express. Because of the delay in time he had arranged, he knew she would be curled up in the luxurious white-linen sheets, waiting for him.

They would make quiet, tender love and save the fiery passion for when they returned from dinner.

He arranged for a room with a two-person jacuzzi tub so they could ignite their passion in the swirling, undulating motion of the scented bubbles, not that they needed any help in that department. All they had to do was see each other.

"Good evening, Mr. Sanders. Your wife is already in the room, waiting," Carly said.

"Thank you," he said as he took the key card.

...Yes, she's waiting for me...

...She will always be waiting...

CHAPTER SIX

Randy

When Randy first opened the Inn, she had no idea, that more often than not, the Inn would be filled to capacity. The Inn had been closed for two years before she purchased it and prior to the foreclosure it had developed a very questionable reputation. The management let things slide and their once-thriving business deteriorated to the point where they eventually went bankrupt.

Randy figured she would be fighting an uphill battle to restore the Inn to its five-star status and was prepared for it to take at least a year or two for that to happen.

No one could have been more than

surprised than Randy when it was up and running within the first six months.

Check-in was at 4 and most guests arrived within the first hour. Randy knew that one of the most important things to make the Inn a success was the guests' first impression. She knew it was extremely important they were treated courteously and not feel rushed when they registered.

Randy knew she was right when she chose Carly for the job. With her sweet, bubbly personality and attention to detail, the guests loved her.

Randy had Reuben work with Carly at the front desk during the busiest check-in times. It could have been chaotic, but they worked so well together that the process of registering the guests worked like clockwork.

When Randy hired him as her assistant, she had full confidence he could be trained in all aspects of running the Inn and she was right. He was her righthand man and functioned in any capacity she needed him to.

She knew she could rely on him completely and he never let her down. Neither did Carly. They were like two peas in a pod and often finished each other's sentences.

Randy thought what a great couple they would make together. They were best friends and often went to the movies or out to eat after work. She knew how Reuben felt about Carly and hoped maybe someday she would see him as someone other than just a friend. Sometimes life worked out like that, and then again, sometimes it didn't.

"Reuben, the Ashworths have a reservation downstairs tonight and I want you to make sure everything is extra special for them. Put them at number six. I ordered a special flower arrangement for the table. Check with Carl, he has the info."

When she first opened the Inn, Randy didn't want to deal with the added hassle and potential failure of having an on-site restaurant. But it became apparent from guests' input, they wanted the option of having dinner without leaving the romantic atmosphere of the Inn.

Just as she did before buying the Inn, she researched the feasibility, both physically and financially, of opening a small dining room. There was a large area in close proximity to the kitchen that she decided would do nicely as a dinner venue. It had been used for storage by the previous owners and would need quite a bit of work to transform it into a restaurant.

With Reuben's help, Randy cleared it out and decided how she wanted to remodel it. There was room enough for eight tables and she figured eight would be a manageable number. It would be small and intimate. She chose to decorate the room in pastel shades of cream and light green with tan and pale pink accents. She piped in a gas fireplace for a romantic atmosphere.

She inquired at the culinary department of the local university for a soon-to-be graduate who was interested in eventually opening a restaurant. Randy was a firm believer in supporting local talent and helping someone else to achieve their goals.

After all, that's how she ended up owning the Inn in the first place.

She interviewed several, capable young people, but as soon as she met Zach, she knew he was the one. He was graduating near the top of his class, but that wasn't what impressed her. He had a contagious enthusiasm and her instinct told her he could help make a success of the restaurant they were going to create from scratch.

As always, Randy was right. Besides his skill for running the business end of a restaurant, he was an incredible chef. He was talented, creative and innovative. He spent months testing different recipes until he was completely satisfied.

Randy, Carly and Reuben were thrilled to have him on board because they were his taste-test dummies. Every day they would sample a new creation, every one a culinary masterpiece.

Randy marveled that such a young, relatively inexperienced chef could be so masterful. She learned that he developed a passion for cooking when he was just seven. His mother was an excellent amateur chef who loved to have her young son as an assistant in the kitchen.

She taught him every aspect of cooking, and much

to the disappointment of his father who wanted him to go to law school and follow in his footsteps, she encouraged him to follow his dream and go to culinary school.

It took eight months to ready the restaurant to open. Zach interviewed a bevy of potential waitstaff. They really only needed one waiter or waitress to staff such a small dining room, but his and Randy's vision for the restaurant was for it to be an upscale, fine-dining experience for the guests. And for that to happen, each waiter or waitress was to have no more than four tables at a time.

Zack hired a young, talented sous-chef who was eager to please and Zack was confident in his ability. They practiced working together, over and over...and over again, until they worked like a finely-tuned instrument. Only then did Zach feel they were ready to tackle the task of putting their combined culinary talents to the test.

Finally, the much-awaited night arrived. Each table had a white linen tablecloth, white taper candles and a crystal bud vase with a single, pink sweetheart rose. The lights were dimmed and the fireplace lit. Romantic music was playing quietly in the background.

They opened on a Thursday night when the Inn was only at half-occupancy due to a predicted, upcoming storm. Randy and Zach were as nervous as two newlyweds on their wedding night. Randy decided to give complementary dinners to eight couples staying at the Inn. She chose those guests who were there for a romantic getaway, thinking they would be the most appreciative and receptive to the gesture.

Everything was in place when the first couple arrived. They staggered the reservations, giving each table sufficient time to order their drinks and peruse the menu before the next guests arrived.

Randy had the waiters, dressed in their crisp, white shirts and black vest and tie, give each table a complementary carafe of wine. Zach knew Randy was doing everything in the dining room to successfully woo the customers. Now it was up to him. As important as ambiance and service were, it was the food that would make or break them.

He held his breath as he sent out the first few entrees, praying the guests would be happy. As any chef in a fine-dining establishment, he went from table to table asking if they were enjoying their meals. He was young and inexperienced and didn't kid himself. Everything was riding on his skill as a chef.

He could feel the dampness under the rim of his chef's hat as he approached the first table.

He needn't have worried. Every table gushed over the exquisite presentation and extraordinary flavor of their meals. Randy hugged him as he returned to the kitchen, beaming with pride.

"We did it, Randy!" he exclaimed.

"No, Zach. *You* did it. I just did the window dressing."

"It's just the first night and all these people had free dinners...and wine. Let's see what it's like tomorrow when they're sober and have to pay for their meals," he chuckled.

Randy laughed too, but she had full

confidence in Zach and knew she made the right decision in giving this young man the monumental task of opening a restaurant. It was a gamble to trust he could do it, but her gamble paid off.

From that time forward, the dining room was full every night due to the glowing reviews of the customers. When guests checked in, they would be asked if they wanted to book a table for dinner. The locals heard about the great restaurant in town and started to frequent it, but Randy made sure the Inn's guests had first dibs on reservations.

When the Ashworths arrived at the dining room, they were greeted by Carl, the Maitre D'.

"We have a reservation. The name's Ashworth" the little, old man with the thick English accent said.

"Yes, Mr. Ashworth, follow me, please," Carl said graciously.

He led them to table number six, a cozy corner table near the fireplace.

He pulled out Mrs. Ashworth's chair and placed the white linen napkin on her lap.

As he handed them the gold-embossed, leather menus, he wished them happy anniversary.

"Thank you," they said in unison.

"This is just lovely," she said as she read the card attached to the flower centerpiece.

Randy stopped by the table to congratulate them on their 70th anniversary. She wished them many more to come, but Mrs. Ashworth was so frail and fragile, Randy was afraid it might be their last.

She would have loved to know about their life together. They must have such stories to tell, a lifetime of stories. But Randy knew she would never be privy to them because they were a dignified, private couple. She suspected they wouldn't share their secrets with anyone. In their generation, it simply wasn't done. You took the good with the bad and with no complaints.

It was really a shame. The world could learn so much from them.

CHAPTER SEVEN

Room# 110 … *Edward and Margaret Ashworth*

Edward Ashworth was a reserved, stiff upper lipped, elderly British gentleman in his late eighties. He was tall and thin with a shock of thick, snow-white hair and deep worry lines etched in his face. There was a lifetime of history to be told from those lines, if he were so inclined to tell the stories behind them. But he wasn't. They were locked behind his cold, unemotional, British facade.

It was only with his beloved wife of seventy years that those stories were shared, because it was *their* stories, the ones they lived through together.

Edward fell in love with Margaret in April

of 1940. She was an usherette at the Rex Cinema in Coventry and he worked in the nearby Daimler Factory that produced gun turrets for British aircraft. He had not yet turned eighteen, so he was unable to join the army for another seven months. The most he could do was help produce the aircraft parts that aided in the war effort until he was of age.

It took Edward months before he worked up the courage to ask Margaret out on a date. There was no hesitation on her part. They were both shy and did little more than smile at each other every Saturday night when he went to the cinema to see whatever movie was playing. He didn't care what movie it was because he wasn't there to watch it. He was there to watch Margaret.

Margaret Billings had just turned seventeen and she was a beauty. She was small and delicate with sparkling, blue eyes. She had dark brown hair that curled in soft waves around her face and cascaded to her shoulders. She had creamy, white skin with a smattering of freckles across her turned-up nose. Unlike other girls, she didn't wear lipstick. She didn't need to. Her lips were a natural rosy color that matched the color in her cheeks whenever she saw Edward.

Their first date was a picnic in the park. She packed a basket of sausage rolls, tea cakes and two bottles of orange squash.

They were both so shy that they barely said two words to each other while they ate. Margaret stared down at her lap, afraid to look up because she didn't know what to say.

Finally, she looked up when she reached into the basket to offer him a tea cake. She gazed at him briefly with her piercing blue eyes and Edward was completely disarmed.

"You're beautiful," he blurted out.

Margaret blushed a deep red, lowered her head and stared at blanket they were sitting on.

"I...I'm sorry," Edward said apologetically.

He hadn't meant to embarrass her. He didn't know what came over him, but he had to say *something*. Even though it was true, it wasn't what he planned to say, but at least it broke the ice.

She looked up, smiling shyly. No one had

ever told her she was beautiful before.

They started to talk.

Do you like working at the cinema? What do you do at the munitions plant? Where do you live? Do you have any brothers or sisters?

After an hour of small talk, they started talking about other things. More serious things.

Are you going to join the army as soon as you turn eighteen? Are you afraid to go to war? Do you know anyone who has been there?

Edward shared that, yes, was joining up right away; no, he wasn't afraid; yes, his older brother was in the 7th Armoured Division in Africa.

Margaret shared her wish to go to nursing school like her sister who had just graduated; yes, she was afraid of the war and for her two older brothers who were serving in the army corps; yes, she hoped to get married someday and have children.

The sun was setting by the time they exhausted all topics of conversation and knew for a fact, they had fallen in love.

In wartime, it wasn't an unusual occurrence

to fall in love quickly and make plans for a future that might never come to fruition. Many marriages were made in haste before a soldier went off to the front with no guarantee he would ever come back.

So when Edward turned eighteen, and before he signed up for the army, they were wed. Margaret was only seventeen, but her parents had no objections. They believed Edward was an upright young man with honorable intentions. Young love in wartime had an urgency about it and her parents understood that. They only hoped their daughter wouldn't be left a young widow, or worse, have to spend her life caring for an emotionally broken or physically disabled casualty of war.

The newly-wed Ashworths spent a brief honeymoon in nearby Stoneleigh and then returned to Coventry to set up house. They found a small flat near Margaret's parents, located between a munitions factory and the local shops. Edward's parents, who lived outside the city limits, contributed some pieces of furniture that were collecting dust in their attic. Margaret's parents gifted them the all-important bed and dresser and Margaret's grandmother hand-stitched curtains for them made of delicate, white-lace and embroidered them with small, pink roses.

They had almost a month before Edward had to report for duty so they did all the things a young couple would do if they had to live a lifetime in a matter of weeks.

They went for long walks and picnics. They went to see the latest movies and eat licorice twists in the back row. They went to the pub to hear the local bands play lively music. But their favorite thing to do was to walk the five miles to the outskirts of the city to the Coventry dance hall.

They were young and in love, so a ten mile trek was not a hardship. They held hands and dreamt about the future. They would buy a little cottage in Burton Green after the war. Edward would continue at the Daimler Factory that would return to producing car engines instead of aircraft parts. She would work as nurse until they had their first child. Then she would stay home to be a wife and mother. They would have two, maybe three, children — one boy and two girls. Margaret would plant a vegetable garden and have window boxes filled with violets and begonias.

Yes, they talked of many wonderful things on their long walks to the dance hall. Once there, they would dance the Jitterbug and then hold each other and sway to the music of Jimmy Dorsey.

Edward and Margaret were determined to cram every bit of life they could, into making memories that would last forever.

Edward was scheduled to report for duty on November 15th. They wanted to spend their last night together dancing in each other's arms, but once they were there, they realized that what they *really* wanted was to go home to their little flat with the white-lace curtains and hold each other until dawn.

As they were leaving to walk home, they heard a lightning storm in the distance. Edward hadn't brought an umbrella and was worried that Margaret would get wet and catch cold, but he needn't have worried.

It wasn't a storm they heard in the distance. Instead, what they saw was the sky filled with hundreds of German bombers dropping high-explosive, incendiary bombs all over the city.

"Oh, Edward!" Margaret screamed. "What is it? What's happening??"

They had heard of the London Blitz just months before, when the Germans bombed London night after night, destroying the city. Thousands of people had been killed and thousands of homes and buildings were demolished. But how could this be happening in Coventry?

"Edward! Our families! Our home!"

Margaret started to cry.

Edward grabbed her hand and they started to run.

They were more than halfway home when Margaret lost her shoe. Debris was floating in the wind and the air was thick with smoke and ash. As she bent down to pick up her shoe, she screamed. Laying at her feet was a small piece of singed white lace with pink roses on it.

"Oh my God!"

She left her shoe and they kept running.

As they got closer, they could see that

Coventry was engulfed in flames. The bombers still filled the sky, dropping an endless supply of explosives.

Margaret and Edward felt helpless. They were at the edge of the city and knew it was futile to go any further. They knew they would most likely be killed if they tried to reach their families, so they just held on tightly to each other and prayed. They prayed that the bombing would stop. They prayed that their families were still alive. They prayed that it was all just a horrible nightmare.

It turned out it *was* a nightmare, but not one from which anyone would wake up. The carnage and terror lasted until just after midnight when the planes dissipated just as suddenly as they had appeared.

The city was still ablaze as they made their way through the wreckage towards their flat. They knew that the singed remnant of the lace curtain they found meant their home had been destroyed. But they didn't care about that. Their only concern was the safety of their families.

Street after street was strewn with wounded and dead bodies amongst the debris. Firefighters were desperately attempting to extinguish the fires, but there simply wasn't enough of them. The telephone lines and electrical wires were intentionally damaged by the bombs which were meant to incapacitate an already crippled city.

When they reached their street, they stopped cold in their tracks. There was practically nothing left. Frozen in place, they saw that almost every building was reduced to burning piles of rubble. People were huddled together in shock, sobbing and wailing in terror and torment. Edward led Margaret towards what had once been their home, looking desperately at the ash-covered, tear-stained faces for anyone they knew.

"Please, please, let them be alive," Margaret whispered to herself.

Edward heard her plea and squeezed her hand tighter. He was afraid of what they were going to find.

"Margaret!!" she heard a voice call out.

"*Mum!!*" she said and ran into her mother's

arms.

Her mother was shaking and sobbing. Margaret was clutching her so tightly, her mother could barely breathe.

"Oh, my God. Oh, my God," her mother said through her sobs.

"Margaret, you're alive. You're alive. You're alive."

She kept repeating herself over and over.

"Yes, Mum, we are," she said as she cried.

"Mum...where's...where's Dad? Where's... where's...Gram?"

Margaret's mother's eyes glazed over.

"They're gone," she whispered.

"Oh, Mum, no! *It can't be! Please* tell me it's not true, Mum."

She was sobbing. Edward put his arms around her.

In a matter of hours, their lives and the lives of everyone in Coventry were changed forever. The Germans targeted their city because it housed many vital munitions factories. Unfortunately, the factories were interspersed with the residential areas. Hundreds of civilians were killed, hundreds wounded, and thousands of buildings destroyed.

Dazed and in a stupor, Edward led his wife and mother-in-law through the carnage towards the outskirts of the city, towards where his parents lived. It was difficult navigating through the debris-strewn streets filled with people screaming and crying.

Edward felt a lump rise up in his throat. He prayed that his parents' home lay outside the line of fire.

The closer they got to the edge of city, the more hopeful he became. The bombing was concentrated in the heart of the city, so his neighborhood was miraculously untouched by the devastation.

It was like day and night. There were hundreds of homes destroyed and people wounded and killed just a short distance away.

His parents were in a state of hysteria, thinking Edward and Margaret had been killed. His mother fell into his arms when arrived at their doorstep. Margaret's mother collapsed and Edward carried her to the sofa. Margaret was crying uncontrollably.

As the night wore on, they could see the fires still blazing in the distance, but there was an eerie calmness that settled on the city. As daylight approached and the full scope of the carnage was realized, the people, in their grief and mourning, came to life. Their shock and terror turned to anger, anger against the Germans. And their anger turned to resolve. This was war, but they would not be beaten. Their stalwart English stoicism would come to the forefront and they would persevere and survive. They had done it once before. The memories of the first World War still loomed large in their minds.

It was decided that Margaret and her mother would remain with the Ashworths. In reality, they had nowhere else to go. They would grieve their losses together, but their wounds would never fully heal.

The most inconceivable thing of all was that Edward had to report for duty that very morning...the morning after the worst night of their lives.

Margaret, still reeling from the loss of her family, watched as her husband packed his duffel bag and left to report for duty. She didn't know if it was going to be last time she would ever see him. Up until the Blitz the night before, the war wasn't real to her, but now there was the stark reality of unmerciful mass killings and butchery. It was almost more than Margaret could bear, but she knew she needed to be strong and send him off with the notion that she would be all right.

The war escalated into a global affair and Edward served most of his time fighting in the blazing-hot, dry Egyptian desert. Margaret would receive letters months after they were written — letters of love and devotion with no mention of the horrors of war.

It was shortly after Edward left that she discovered she was going to have a baby. She wrote him with the news and he wrote back that it was a gift from God.

No matter what Edward's outcome in the

war, Margaret would always have a piece of him to love and cherish.

For Margaret's mother, nothing could ever replace the loss of her husband and mother, but the birth of a grandchild would ease some of her grief and give her hope for the future.

Edward George Ashworth, named after her husband and father, was born on August 4th, exactly nine months to the day they were married. He was a beautiful, chubby baby with Edward's sandy blond hair and her blue eyes. Margaret sent him a picture of baby Eddie sitting on her lap and he put it in the left hand pocket of his uniform, just above his heart, right next to the picture he had of her from the day they were married. He carried the pictures with him through the years of, what seemed like, endless fighting. They were with him the day he was shot by an Italian sniper.

He felt the searing bullet tear through the flesh of his shoulder, but remembered nothing more until he regained consciousness in a desert field hospital.

His wound was critical. He lost a lot of

blood and much of the mobility of his left arm. After surgery and weeks of recuperation, he was shipped back to an army hospital in London before being discharged and sent home.

Edward told Margaret none of it. He knew she would be in a panic, not knowing the extent of his wounds and what the outcome would be. It wasn't until he was ready for discharge that he wrote and told her he was coming home.

When she received his letter, Margaret cried with both joy and sorrow. Joy for the imminent return of her husband and sorrow for the wounds he suffered.

Most of Coventry had been rebuilt by the time he arrived home, except for the Coventry Cathedral that was burnt to the ground on that fateful night of the Blitz. It was decided to leave the ruins intact as a painful reminder of their tragic losses.

Until the day he died, he would never forget the way she looked when he saw her standing in the doorway of their house. She was wearing a cornflower-blue cotton dress, the exact color of her eyes. Her dark hair was cut short with curls framing her face. She was holding Eddie in her arms, his blond curls in stark contrast to hers.

He was wriggling to get out of her arms. She set him down and went running towards her husband. She threw her arms around him and he kissed her so hard it took her breath away.

"Oh, Edward. I missed you so. I was so afraid you would never come home."

She gently touched his left arm that was still housed in a sling.

"Does it hurt much?"

He lied and said it didn't. He bent down to tousle little Eddie's blonde curls.

It would be several years before he regained enough strength and mobility to pick up his son.

The following years were lean ones. Rationing made it difficult to have the daily necessities of food, clothes, soap and petrol, but they managed, as did everyone else. It was a luxury to have a breakfast of bacon, toast and eggs with the meager allowances they were allotted each week. Margaret planted a "victory garden" so they at least had vegetables to go with the small quantities of meat they were able to get with their coupon books.

As the years went by and the war ended, rationing began to ease. By the time Eddie was eleven, most items became available again. Margaret was thrilled, that for the first time, she had enough sugar and flour to bake him a beautiful birthday cake with blue and yellow frosting.

Edward returned to work at the factory and eventually, after the war ended, became an automotive engineer. The Ashworths decided to emigrate to the United States and take up residence in Michigan where Edward began to work for General Motors.

Tragically, their son was killed in an auto accident at the age of twenty-two. It was certainly not the first loss they suffered, but it was, by far, the worst. They loved their son beyond measure and never fully recovered from his death.

There was never any question that their marriage wouldn't survive. They made it through the horrible tragedies of war, weathered the post-war hardships and buried their beloved son.

They had a lifetime of adversity, but they also had a lifetime of love and devotion.

The love that started out as a youthful romance, blossomed into a life of courage and dedication that would withstand whatever life threw at them. They knew that love wasn't a feeling, it was a commitment...no matter what.

Now here it was, seventy years later, and the love and devotion they felt was no less than it was the day they married. Their bodies were failing, but their love never would.

It was a forever love, for however long that was going to be.

CHAPTER EIGHT

Room# 211 ... *The Honeymoon Suite*

Randy had the room beautifully arranged – a crystal vase with a dozen red roses, a chilled bottle of champagne, the bed turned down with chocolate truffles on the pillows, the lights dimmed and soft music playing.

It was all ready for a very special night.

Randy was with Carly at the front desk when Michael and Hannah Kelly arrived.

"Congratulations," she said as she smiled at them.

"Thank you," they said in unison.

They looked like two scared rabbits caught

stealing carrots from someone's vegetable garden.

"I'll have your luggage brought up," Carly said as she handed them the keycard.

"Oh, that's...that's okay. We don't have very much," he told her.

Hannah, his new bride, blushed and looked down at the floor.

He took the keycard and the two small, mismatched suitcases. Randy and Carly watched them walk down the hall towards their room, Michael carrying the bags, Hannah close by his side.

"Poor kids," Randy said.

"What do you mean?"

"I don't think they have a pot to piss in."

"What makes you think that?"

"When he called for the reservation, he asked for our cheapest room rates. I asked if it was a special occasion and he said it was their honeymoon. He sounded embarrassed when I asked for a credit card to hold the reservation. He said he didn't have one and asked if they could pay for the room when they arrived."

"I was wondering about that. Nobody pays with cash and he gave me all tens and twenties."

Carly looked at Randy and chuckled.

"*So*...what did you do?"

"I upgraded them to the honeymoon suite. If they're hurting for money, they're going to have it tough enough. I think they should at least have a special wedding night to remember."

Carly laughed.

"You're such a sucker for a sob story."

Randy sighed. Carly was right. She had a great deal of empathy for people struggling to get by. She had been there once herself.

At that moment the in-house phone rang. It was room 211. Carly picked up the receiver.

"Front desk. How can I help you, Mr. Kelly?"

"I'm afraid there's some mistake."

"What do you mean?"

"We're in the wrong room."

"No, Mr. Kelly. It's the right room. It's the honeymoon suite."

He started to stutter and Carly knew he was embarrassed.

"But, but...we didn't ask for it. We asked for one of your...your...smaller rooms."

"Oh, I'm *so* sorry for the inconvenience. They were all taken. We had to upgrade you to the suite. I hope you don't mind. Of course, there's no extra charge."

She was smiling at Randy as she lied to him.

"But there's flowers and champagne... and..."

"Oh, yes. That's complimentary for the honeymoon suite."

She could tell he was speechless on the other end of the line. Then he whispered, almost inaudibly, "thank you very much."

"Hannah, you won't believe it."

"What?"

She was sitting in the chair by the door, jacket still on, ready to leave when Michael found out what room they were *really* supposed to be in.

"This is our room!"

"What do you mean? It can't be. We can't afford this room. We can't afford to be here at *all*."

"They said the smaller rooms were taken and apologized that they had to upgrade us to the honeymoon suite!"

"No way. Are you *kidding* me?"

He shook his head and she started to cry.

Michael took her in his arms and stroked her soft, chestnut hair. He lifted her face and kissed her gently. It was like a dream come true.

Hannah had been very upset that Michael used some of his savings for their wedding night. She was perfectly happy to spend the night in the new apartment they were moving into.

Between the two of them, Hannah was the practical one. She came from a family who lived paycheck-to paycheck and struggled when any unexpected expenses came up. When she married, and she always knew it was going to be Michael, she wanted a different kind of life. She didn't expect to be rich, but she didn't want to struggle every day just to have the basics. She didn't want her children to wear hand-me-downs and have to stand on the free-lunch line at school. She grew up being embarrassed that she wasn't "as good as" the other kids at school. Girls could be so cruel and she was teased because she didn't wear expensive boots or the latest-style jeans. She didn't want *her* children to feel the same way.

Hannah fell in love with Michael when they were in high school and always knew they would marry someday, but she wanted it to be when they could live better lives than her parents had.

Michael had been assistant manager of produce at a local supermarket and was just promoted to assistant manager of the entire store. He calculated that with the increase in salary, they could marry. Money would be tight, but they would make ends meet.

It wasn't the way Hannah planned on it. When she dreamt about them getting married, there was a long, white wedding dress, a church full of flowers and no worries about the future.

But accidents happened and they couldn't wait. When Hannah missed her first period, she didn't think much of it because she had always been irregular and they always took precautions. But when she missed the second, she knew she might be pregnant.

When she told Michael, he picked her up and twirled her around.

"That's fantastic," he said as he put her down and hugged her tightly.

He was thrilled that they were going to have a baby. He wasn't the practical one and he saw nothing but happiness for their future. He didn't know the reservations Hannah had about marrying before he had a good enough, and secure enough, job.

He ran right out and bought a pregnancy test. They sat together and watched the little line turn blue. He was grinning ear to ear. She, however, felt a lump in her throat and her heart skipped a beat. But his excitement was contagious and within a few minutes she was as happy as he was. She quickly put aside the financial fears she had. With all the naïvety that comes with the inexperience of youth, they started planning for the perfect life they were going have.

Hannah didn't tell her parents that she was pregnant, nor did Michael tell his. They decided to elope quietly, and tell them when they returned… after their one-night honeymoon. They knew Hannah's parents would be thrilled because they loved Michael as if he were the son they never had. *They* never had much in life, materialistically speaking, so it didn't bother them that their daughter probably wouldn't either.

Michael's parents would feel differently. *They* had high hopes that after Michael graduated, he would go to college and "make something of himself." Instead, he went to work in, what they considered, a dead-end job. They didn't think working as a store manager, no matter what the salary potential was, comparable to a white collar profession. Michael's father worked as a factory supervisor his entire adult life and even though he made enough money for them to live very comfortably, he wanted something more for his son. But Michael was only an average student and knew college would be a struggle and it just wasn't for him. Besides, he didn't want to put his life on hold for four or five years. Michael wanted to get on with the business of living. He wanted to marry

Hannah.

On their wedding night, they planned to go to dinner at an inexpensive tavern. Michael wanted to take her to a romantic restaurant with candlelight and soft music, but Hannah was adamant that they had already spent more than enough money on the room. Besides, she felt anywhere could be romantic, as long as they were together. He capitulated to make her happy.

Hannah was just changing out of the cream-colored dress she wore as a "wedding gown" to put on jeans and a sweater when the phone rang.

"Mr. Kelly, I'm so sorry to disturb you, but I forgot to mention there's a complimentary dinner in our dining room that is included as part of the honeymoon package. If you wish to take advantage of it, I could make the reservation for you," Carly said as she smiled deviously.

There was silence on the other end of the line.

"Mr Kelly?"

"Uh, yes...yes...that would be great."

"They have an opening at seven-thirty.

Would that be okay?"

"Absolutely," he answered.

He hung up the phone and turned to Hannah.

"Put your dress back on," he said.

She looked at him with a puzzled look.

He just smiled and thought…no matter what the future would hold, their first night together as husband and wife would be something they would never forget…what an unbelievable gift from God this all was.

…they wouldn't ever know where the gift really came from…

CHAPTER NINE

Randy

Randy glanced into the dining room on her way to the office. She smiled as she saw "Mr. and Mrs." Kelly whispering and holding hands across the table. Sweet, young, innocent love. She tried to remember what that felt like, but those feelings were long-since dead and buried.

Carly thought she was a softy, and she was. But it was more than that. She was just paying it forward and she knew Jimmy would be pleased.

She felt her cell phone buzz in her pocket. She moved out of earshot of the dining room.

"Yes, Carly."

"Randy, I need you to come to the front

desk, right away," she said with urgency in her voice.

Uh-oh. I wonder what fire I have to put out, she thought.

She hurried up the stairs and headed towards the lobby. As she approached the front desk, she saw Carly grinning. She stopped cold in her tracks.

"Noah!" she yelled and ran to throw her arms around her son.

He hugged her back.

"Surprise!"

"What are you *doing* here?"

She was still holding onto him and there were tears in her eyes.

"Well, I was in the neighborhood," he joked.

"No, seriously. What *are* you doing here?"

She was still in a state of shock. She hadn't seen him for over eight months.

He laughed.

"Well, if you don't want to see me, I can always go back..."

"Over my dead body you will!"

She hugged him again.

"I just can't believe you're here. God, I'm so happy to see you. Are you here on business?"

"Nope."

"Well, are you going to tell my why?"

"Nope."

"Noah!"

"Sorry, mom. You're just gonna have to wait."

"Wait for *what*? C'mon, Noah. You're driving me crazy."

"Well, I consider that a great honor."

"You consider *what* a great honor?"

"Driving you crazy," he said as he chuckled.

Carly was watching from the desk and started to crack up. Randy turned and looked at her.

"Did you know about this?"

"My lips are sealed."

Randy feigned a scowl.

"You're both fired."

"Awesome. Carly, want to go grab a bite to eat?"

"Will you two please *stop* it."

"Okay, Mom. I came to take you out to dinner."

"Dinner? Seriously? You flew three thousand miles for dinner."

"Well, you do have the best rack of lamb in the country."

Randy punched him lightly on the arm, then hugged him again.

"I don't care *why* you're here. I've just missed you so much."

Noah lived and worked in Los Angeles as a biophysicist. Randy couldn't tell you exactly what he did or what his Doctoral degree was about because she didn't understand a word of it. He was brilliant and when he started talking science, she would zone out and wonder where the hell he got his smarts from. It wasn't from her. She was bright, above average, but not anywhere close to his level. And he *certainly* didn't get anything from his deadbeat father.

So she would sit and politely listen to him

discuss his research on the environmental impact of the molecular structure of some microorganism. Whatever. She was just so very proud of him.

He had his head screwed on straight and she felt so grateful that it had never been, even remotely, on crooked.

As far as Noah was concerned, Randy was the perfect mother. She had worked hard to provide for him when he was growing up and he knew that wasn't easy. His father abandoned them when he was a baby and he knew Randy sacrificed much of her life for him. Every morning at four-thirty she went to work — in the dark, in the cold, in the snow, driving an old broken-down car that her friend Jimmy kept on the road for her. He never saw her buy new clothes or go out with friends or on a date. Her whole life revolved around him.

He knew she couldn't afford to send him to college, so he worked weekends and after school to help with tuition. He earned several, partial academic scholarships, but knew it wouldn't cover everything. He felt guilty that Randy fully intended to take out any necessary loans he needed so he could go to the college of his choice. She wasn't about to deprive her son of the education he wanted and more importantly, deserved. His father was a scumbag and there was no way in hell Randy was going to let that hold Noah back.

When his father, Kevin, took off and left them, he never looked back. They moved in with his grandmother so Randy could provide for him. His Nana babysat when Randy worked the long, tedious hours at the coffeehouse and she stepped in as a second mother when Randy couldn't be there. It wasn't until he was seven that he first asked about his father.

Randy dreaded the day she would have to have "the talk." She dreaded it even more than the one she would have to have someday about sex.

She was kind and gracious to the memory of the bum who abandoned his son. He left and was never heard from again. She could have maligned him so Noah would grow up hating him, but that's not what Randy wanted…not for Kevin's sake, but for Noah's. He didn't deserve to have his spirit crushed and live his life with his heart filled with hate.

So she told him the gentlest version of the story she could think of — he loved his son, but didn't think he would be a good enough father. He felt Noah would be better off without him. It was a simple enough story for a seven year-old to understand. It wasn't until he was in his early teens that he wanted, needed, a better explanation. By then, he was mature enough to hear the full story. He was angry, not so much for himself, since he never knew the man, but for his mother who was hurt and devastated by him. Noah never asked about him again. He never wanted to find his father and hoped his father never wanted to find him. It was a closed book, one he *never* wanted to open.

And now he was a grown man living the life that made him happy. He had a career that he loved, lived in the city of angels where the sun shone almost every day, and had a rich, full social life.

Noah was twenty-eight and as far as Randy knew, he no longer had a love interest in his life. At least he never talked about one. He had been in a two year, very rocky relationship with the girl he intended to marry. It hadn't ended well and Randy suspected his emotions were still a little raw.

“Where are your bags?” she asked.

“Reuben hid them in the storeroom.”

“Let’s get them and we can take them to my room.”

“That’s okay. We can do it later. Why don’t you go get changed?”

She looked down at what she was wearing and decided she definitely needed to spiff up.

“Okay, c’mon,” Randy said as she walked towards her apartment.

She had taken several of the Inn’s rooms to fashion a small apartment for herself. She didn’t need a full kitchen, since she hated to cook, so she just put in a mini-fridge, hotplate and microwave. She made one room into a bedroom and the other into a small, but comfortable living room with a sleeper sofa for Noah when he came to visit.

“I’ll wait here. I want to catch up with

Reuben and Carly."

"Okay. I'll be right back. Don't be giving away any secrets, Carly," she said as she winked at Noah.

When she'd gone, Noah asked Carly if everything was all set.

She grinned and nodded.

"Absolutely."

The game was on.

Randy came back dressed in a pair of black dress slacks and a powder-blue, satin blouse. Noah smiled.

"You look beautiful, Mom."

He thought what a shame it was that such an attractive woman lived her life alone. She had so much to give and no one to give it to.

They went downstairs to the dining room.

"Noah, so good to see you again," Carl said and shook his hand.

"Hey, Carl how's it going?"

"Pretty good, but my boss is a real ballbuster," he said as he looked at Randy and laughed.

"Yeah, she always has been."

Randy elbowed him in the ribs.

"Knock it off you two. C'mon, I'm starving. With all this excitement, I've worked up quite an appetite," she said and slid her arm through his.

"Right this way, *madame*," Carl said as he bowed and waved them towards the dining room.

He led them to a table for two in the corner so they could talk privately. As he pulled out Randy's chair, Noah spoke up.

"No. No, I don't like this table," he said and took Randy by the arm.

He turned her around and they were facing a table where there was a man and woman sitting, engrossed in conversation.

"I want to sit over there," he said.

Puzzled, Randy looked up at him as if to say, what the hell?

As he led her closer to the table, the couple rose.

"Mom, I would like you to meet Jennifer, my fiancée, and her father Jack Adams."

He smiled as he watched his mother's face

run the gamut of emotions in a nanosecond. First, confusion, then surprise, then shock, and lastly... complete joy.

"Oh my, *God!* Noah!"

Randy threw her arms around his neck and hugged him tightly. Then she turned to Jennifer.

"Jennifer," she cried and wrapped her arms around her.

"I'm so glad to finally meet you, Mrs. Arnold," Jennifer said.

"Oh, call me, Randy, *please*. Or even Mom if you want to."

"See, I told you. You had nothing to worry about," Noah said to his fiancée.

"She was scared to death to meet you," he told his mother.

"Scared? Scared of *me*?" Randy said as she squeezed Jennifer's hand. "Sweetheart, I have been waiting for a moment like this for a long time. I was beginning to think it was *never* going to happen."

Noah rolled his eyes and laughed.

"Good *grief*, Randy," he said with mock-sarcasm. "I'm not even thirty yet."

"Don't call me Randy," she said.

From the time he was in his teens, he called her Randy whenever he wanted to tease her. She pretended to hate it, but it was just the opposite.

"Oh, I'm so sorry, Mr. Adams. In the excitement, I completely forgot about you," Randy said and reached across the table to shake his hand.

He laughed.

"Jack, please, and I understand. I was just as surprised when Jen showed up on my doorstep last night to spring the news on me."

"So you didn't know either? Well, it makes me feel a little better that I wasn't the only one left out of the loop. I can't stand being loop-less."

"No, these two have managed to keep this whole thing a secret."

"Okay, so you've kept us in the dark long enough. Spill it. Tell us everything," Randy said.

"Can't we have dinner first? I thought you were starving."

She laughed.

"For some strange reason, I'd forgotten all about it."

"Well, I haven't."

Noah nodded to the waiter who had been standing by, waiting for a signal. He went into the kitchen and came back with Zach.

"Noah! Congratulations, buddy," he said and shook his hand. "And this must be Jennifer. I'm pleased to meet you. Noah has told me so much about you."

"You mean *you* knew all about this?" Randy asked.

"Sure. Noah called me last month to make arrangements for a special dinner, fit for a king and queen, he told me. I had a hell of a time keeping the secret. Came close to spilling the beans a couple of times."

Randy just shook her head. It was still spinning from the news.

As anxious as Randy and Jack were to hear all the details, Noah insisted they have their dinner first.

Zach did her proud. He created a magnificent feast for them using every skill he had, literally from soup to nuts and everything in between — Beluga caviar on petit-point toast, cream of curried cauliflower soup, a limoncello sorbet to cleanse the palate, poached salmon with basil-lime coulis served over brown-butter risotto, sliced poached pear with roquefort cheese, and then for the finishing touch…bananas flambé with hand-churned, Madagascar vanilla-bean ice cream topped with finely crushed almonds.

Zach spent the entire month planning and practicing the menu until he created what he considered the perfect combination of exquisite taste and presentation.

His supreme efforts were not wasted. Every course was better than the last.

"I've eaten in many fine restaurants over the years," Jack said, " but I don't think I have ever had a more exceptional meal. Kudos to the Chef."

Randy found it hard to contain herself and not jump up and hug Zach for his outstanding effort and achievement.

"I'm so glad you were pleased," Zach said.

He was beaming ear-to-ear when he returned to the kitchen.

"Okay, can you put us out of our misery now?" Randy asked.

Noah laughed and Jennifer smiled.

"Oh, I suppose so," he said as he took Jennifer's hand in his.

"We've been friends for years, but we were always out of sync when it came to taking it to the next level. When I was with Andrea, Jen was working on her doctorate. When Andrea and I broke up, Jen was dating Max and neither of us knew how we really felt about each other."

Randy saw him squeeze Jen's hand a little tighter.

"Then six months ago, the pieces just fell into place. We were having coffee in my apartment and my hand accidentally brushed against hers... and the rest is history."

Jennifer leaned her head on his shoulder and the chemistry between them was palpable.

Randy and Jack sat and listened to their story and when it was finished, they both felt the same way. They were perfect for each other.

"So when's the wedding?" Randy asked.

Noah chuckled.

"Didn't I tell you that would be the first thing she'd ask?" he said to Jen.

"Yup, you did."

"So?"

"We figured we'd come back in May or June and have a small ceremony. Jen doesn't have much family and neither do we."

"It's just me and my sister," Jack said. "I'm a widower."

"And it's just me, Mom and my Nana in Florida, but I'm not sure she's up to the trip."

"Are you kidding?" she said. "She wouldn't miss this if she were on her deathbed."

Noah laughed.

"Yeah, you're right."

His Nana had been a very important part of his life and it wouldn't be the same without her.

"We were thinking, a Justice of the Peace at Town Hall and then maybe dinner here afterward."

"I think we can do a little better than that," Randy said. "You can get married here in the gazebo. The trees and flowers will be in bloom and we'll close the dining room for a private party, and..."

"Mom, we said simple."

"That *is* simple. There'll be close to twenty people."

"Twenty? Mom, it's only seven or eight."

"Noah, you don't think you're going to get married without Carly and Reuben, Zach and Angie...and everyone else, do you?"

"Oh. I'm sorry, Mom. I don't know what I was thinking. Of course, you're right. They're all family."

"You bet they are. Now, I figure Zach can prepare the menu and have his assistants do the cooking. Angie can..."

Noah and Jennifer were laughing.

"Okay, okay, I give it up. We'll do it your way," Noah said and threw his hands up in the air.

"Listen, Mom, do you mind if Jen and I cut out for a little while? No offense, but we'd like a little time alone."

"Yeah, I guess you would," she said and chuckled.

"Jack, how about you?" Noah asked politely.

"Go ahead. We'll just finish our coffee and talk about solving the world's problems."

"Thanks," he said and took Jennifer by the hand.

Jack and Randy watched them leave.

"They make a cute couple," he said. "Are you okay with this?"

"Absolutely. Jen's a sweet girl."

"Yes, she is. And Noah seems like a fine young man. I think they'll be happy."

They relaxed and lingered over coffee, talking about their kids and their future.

When they had exhausted the subject, Randy asked how long he had been a widower.

"Over fifteen years. Cancer."

"Oh, I'm very sorry."

"She was just thirty-one. Jen was only ten and it was hard raising a daughter alone."

"How 'bout you? Do you mind me asking?"

"No, I don't mind. Divorced. He left when Noah was a baby. I never heard from him again."

"So you know what it's like to raise a

child by yourself."

"Yes, but I had help. We lived with my mom and I couldn't have done it without her. Did you have anyone to help you?"

"I had my sister, but she lived across the country and had a family of her own. But I called her all the time, especially when Jen turned thirteen. I didn't know what the heck to do with a teenage girl," he said and laughed.

"Yeah, girls are harder than boys at that age. Or so I've heard."

"Yeah, it's all about hormones and drama. I didn't think I would survive, but Jen was a good girl and didn't give me too much trouble. I'm very proud of the woman she's become."

"You should be. You did a good job."

"You, too."

They sat and shared stories about raising their kids and what it was like living alone. They discovered they had much in common and were still talking when the dining room closed.

"I guess we've overstayed our welcome," he said and stood up.

"Hey, no problem. I know the owner," she said and they both laughed.

"Well, I guess the kids will tell us more of the details, tomorrow. Do you know when they're flying home?" Randy asked.

"Sunday, so we have them for a few more days."

"Great. I miss Noah. I don't get to see him very often."

"Same with me."

"Well, I have to get up early. An Innkeeper's job never ends."

"Randy, it was very nice to meet you, and it was under the best of circumstances. Goodnight."

"Goodnight, Jack."

As he left, he looked back and gave her a little wave.

He thought to himself, what a really nice woman.

She waved back and thought, what a really nice man.

CHAPTER TEN

Room# 114

It was one of the few mornings Randy pushed the snooze alarm…twice.

Damn it, she muttered.

The obnoxious cricket sounds of the alarm cut into the dream she didn't want to wake up from. It was the kind of dream you didn't *ever* want to wake up from. A dream of peace, love and harmony — the kind of dream that a hippie from the '60's would relish.

She was hiking up a steep, snow-capped, purple mountain to the summit. It was an easy climb. There was no danger, no struggle. Just the fresh, crisp air and the deep-blue sky.

She could feel the warmth of the sun on her face as she made her way through the wispy, white clouds that enveloped the peak. She stood at the very top of the mountain and looked down on an expanse of bright green, rolling hills. There was a crystal-clear, blue lake, fed by a cascading waterfall streaming down from the sky.

The view was sumptuous and resplendent. The landscape was saturated with every tint and hue from a Crayola box of 64 crayons. The colors were psychedelic and sparkled in the sunlight. A rainbow slashed through the puffy, white clouds that hovered over the velvety, green grass below.

She felt peaceful and still, and bathed in tranquility. She wanted to stay forever on that mountaintop, but she was suddenly whisked away.

She found herself floating on a cottony, white cloud. As she drifted, the valley below disappeared and she set down on a hot, sandy beach. There was a sandcastle that stood fifteen feet high. Children were running in and out of the turrets, blowing bright pink and blue bubbles into the sea breeze.

A large, soapy bubble floated down and swallowed her up. She sat in the bubble watching the children and saw that Noah was one of them. He waved at her and she waved back. He's having so much fun, she thought. She watched him running and laughing and then he grabbed onto a bubble and floated up and away.

He waved at her again and mouthed, I love you, and then he was gone.

She called to him.

"I love you."

"He'll be back," a voice from behind her whispered.

It was calm and convincing.

Someone took her hand and she felt an overwhelming sense of well-being.

At that moment, the rude shrill of the alarm cut in on her reverie.

Randy pushed the snooze alarm to return to the beach.

There were fading glimpses of a man in a raincoat walking beside her. He slipped his arm around her and brushed his lips against hers.

Then those goddamn annoying crickets chirped and woke her again.

No, no, she thought. Not now. Give me just a little more time, but by this time she was fully awake.

It was amazing how a dream could seem so real and make her feel such tranquility and peace. As she showered and dressed, she kept replaying the memory until she finally had to let it go and start her day.

What a great day it was going to be. She'd turn the innkeeper reins over to Reuben so she could spend the day with Noah and Jennifer.

They stayed overnight with Jack and arranged to meet for breakfast at a local diner.

She slipped into jeans, a t-shirt and her favorite sweater. They were her day-off, dress down clothes that she didn't get to wear very often.

By the time she got to the diner, she was breathless. She'd been rushing to get there so she wouldn't waste a single moment of their time together. They were already sitting at a table.

"Sorry," she said as she slid into the empty

seat next to Jack.

"No worries. We just got here ourselves."

The waitress came over with menus and a coffeepot. Simultaneously, they turned over the coffee mugs in front of them and the waitress filled them.

"Hi. My name is Amy. I'll give you a few minutes to look these over," she said as she laid the menus down on the table.

"Thanks," Randy said.

"They make the best buttermilk pancakes," Noah told Jennifer. "Or at least they used to."

"They still do," Randy and Jack said at the same time and started to laugh.

"I eat here all the time," Jack said.

"Unfortunately, I don't get the chance to go out to eat very often. The Inn keeps me pretty busy."

"I'm sure it does, but maybe you could manage to get out once in a while. They serve a mean homemade, chicken potpie for dinner."

Noah nudged Jennifer and she knew just what he was thinking. Wouldn't it be nice.

They ordered breakfast and were engaged in a lively conversation when Randy's cell phone buzzed.

"Damn," she mumbled under her breath.

"This better be important," she said to Reuben, only slightly joking.

She knew it must be, because he could handle almost any crisis without her and he knew she wouldn't want to be interrupted.

"I'm sorry, Randy. You know I wouldn't disturb you if I didn't have to, but I don't know how to handle this."

"I know. What is it?"

"I just got a call from Mercy General. They have a guy who came in and collapsed in the ER. The only thing he had on him was one of our key cards."

"No wallet?"

"No. No identification at all. And since our keycards only have our name on them, the only way I can find out what room he's in and who he is, is if I have the card."

Randy sighed. She knew she was going

to have to go and get it.

"Okay. I'll head over to the hospital and bring it back to you. Then we can give them his information. I hope he's okay, whoever he is."

Randy went back to the table and explained what happened.

"I'm really sorry. This shouldn't take too long."

"Don't worry about it. We have plenty to talk about. We'll be here when you get back," Jack said and smiled at her.

She smiled back. Then she kissed Noah on the forehead and left.

The hospital was just a hop, skip and a jump from the diner so Randy was there in minutes. When she got to the ER, the woman at the registration desk gave her the key card.

"I'll be back in a few minutes. He probably left his wallet in the room."

"Thanks, I appreciate it."

Randy parked in the archway reserved for registering guests. She figured it would only take a minute or two to get the information the hospital needed. She realized, that in her haste, she hadn't asked about his condition and didn't even know if he was dead or alive. She felt a little guilty that she was so preoccupied with being with Noah, she didn't even think about.

"Hey, Randy. I'm sorry. If I had the card I could have done this myself."

"Oh, don't worry. It'll only take a minute. Run it for me and I'll go check the room."

She handed him the card and he ran it through to find the room # and registration info.

Reuben wrote down the information and handed it to her with the keycard.

"Room 114," he told her.

"When did he check in?"

"Last night when you were having dinner with Noah."

"Did he look sick?"

"I don't know. Carly checked him in while you were in the dining room. She's on break. I can go get her."

"No, don't bother her. I'll find out about

him soon enough."

She slipped the paper in her pocket without looking at it and walked down to Room 114.

She swiped the card and opened the door when the light turned green.

It was one of the smaller, less expensive rooms and the only one with twin beds.

Only one of the beds was disturbed and a small suitcase was on the other bed, still packed.

Randy looked on the desk to find his wallet. It had fallen on the floor next to the wastebasket. She picked it up and then saw a thick, white envelope propped up on the desk lamp.

It simply said — Randy.

Odd, she thought.

She picked up the wallet and gasped when she opened it and saw the driver's license.

Kevin O'Malley.

"Oh, my God," she whispered.

Randy had changed back to her maiden name after the divorce so there was no way Carly would have known Kevin was her ex-husband.

Randy picked up the fat envelope and sat

on the bed. Her heart was racing and she felt as though she was going to throw up.

She just stared at it. She was frozen. With what?...fear?...anger? She was in shock and was flooded with a whirlwind of emotions, none of them good.

She pulled out the piece of paper that she'd stuck in her pocket.

Kevin O'Malley. No car. Arrived by taxi. Paid in cash. Staying only one night.

Her hands were shaking and she was barely able to open the envelope.

The letter was several pages long and handwritten. She was afraid to read it, but knew she had to.

Dear Randy,

I know this must be a shock. After thirty years, I'm sure you never expected to hear from me again and I'm sure you never wanted to.

The first and most important thing I have

to say to you is how terribly sorry I am. I can't even imagine the hell you went through when I abandoned you and Noah. I have no explanation and no excuse except that I was a low-life, drunken bum.

I was immature and selfish and all I cared about was myself and what I wanted. And all I wanted was liquor and women.

When I met you, I didn't think you'd even look at me twice. When I asked you out, I had only one thing on my mind and it wasn't marriage. But we did get married and I treated you like crap. When you got pregnant, it scared the shit out of me. All I could think about was getting the hell of there. I didn't want a wife, and certainly not a baby. I just wanted to run around and party. When Ashley got pregnant, I knew it was my way out. I took off and left you with Noah to fend for yourselves, and I never looked back. I wasn't about to be trapped with Ashley, either, so I took off on her, too.

I spent years drinking, partying and womanizing. I spiraled down a slippery slope and eventually got into drugs. Pot led to cocaine and cocaine led to heroine. I was a drug-addicted dirt-

bag and had to turn to crime to support my habit. I stole anything I could sell on the street and started holding up liquor stores and gas stations. I overdosed twice and wished I died because I was living in a hell I couldn't get out of. I tried to get clean a million times and couldn't do it.

Eventually I ended up in prison for dealing and wanted to die. I tried to hang myself, but the guards found me and put me on suicide watch.

That became the turning point of my life. I came so close to death and realized I didn't really want to die, but I was trapped in the darkest hell you could possibly imagine and had no hope.

I'd been in prison for fifteen years and something inside me just broke. I fell to my knees and sobbed. I was desperate. I begged God for help and I didn't even believe in God. But for the first time in my life I saw the tiniest spark of hope.

They got me into a recovery program and I got clean. I really believe it was God who saved me, because there certainly wasn't anything or anybody else in the world who could.

That was two years ago and I've been trying

to put together the pieces of my life ever since. I know there's absolutely nothing I could ever do to make up for the pain and suffering I caused you. And there's certainly nothing I could do to make up for leaving Noah without a father. I know you were both far better off without me. I would have dragged you down into hell with me and I wouldn't have even cared.

I don't have the right to ask for your forgiveness because what I did was unforgivable. But I need to say how sorry I am for all the pain I caused you both. Every single day, I deeply regret the person I was and the horrible choices I made.

I thought about writing Noah a letter, too, but I wouldn't know what to say. All he knows is that I abandoned him and didn't love him. And he's right. I didn't love anything or anyone. I didn't know how to. I didn't know what love was. It took me a lifetime of drowning in a pit of despair to find out.

Randy, you're an incredible woman and you've done a remarkable job raising your son. I can't call him ours because I lost the right to call him mine the day I walked out the door.

I made sure you didn't see me sitting in the

dining room last night. I watched the two of you together and could see how happy you both are. What a fantastic young man he seems to be. I'm sure you are very proud of him and you should be. You raised him by yourself and that had to have been unthinkably hard. My heart is broken because if I was a different man, if I was the man I'm trying to be today, I could have been part of that. It could have been me sitting at that table with you.

I'll be leaving this morning before you have a chance to see me. I would never want to cause you any more suffering than I already have. I just wanted to get a glimpse of you and leave this letter. I never imagined that I would get to see Noah, too. I can only believe that it was God who made that happen.

Randy, I have no right to ask for forgiveness, but if you could find it in your heart, I could die a happy man.

With a heavy, but grateful heart,

Kevin

Randy put the letter down on the bed and hung her head. There were tears streaming down her face. She was speechless. From out of nowhere, the man who'd broken her heart and torn her life apart, showed up and was making amends for the anguish and pain he caused her and Noah.

Her thoughts and emotions were in a jumble. She had feelings of anger, fear, sorrow, regret, and even sympathy. Anger that he showed up in her life, fear that he wanted to involve himself in Noah's life, sorrow and regret for what could have been, and sympathy for the broken man whom she once loved and the pitiable life he had lived.

Randy sat in shock for a few minutes, then shook it off.

She tried to gather her thoughts and figure out what to do. Should she tell Noah? No. There was no way she was going to shake his world to the core with this. Should she see Kevin? No. She would go to the hospital with his ID, drop it off, and leave. She put the letter and his wallet in her purse and left.

"Thank you," the ER receptionist said as Randy handed her Kevin's driver's license and insurance card. "You can have a seat over there. Someone will be out in a moment."

Randy sat in one of the waiting room chairs. She wanted to leave, but something told her to stay. She was feeling the full gamut of her emotions. Did she or didn't she want to see Kevin? Her stomach was twisted in knots.

"Mrs. O'Malley?" a tall, thin man in green scrubs asked her.

"Uh, no. Randy Arnold. I'm his ex-wife," she said, by way of clarification.

"Ah, yes. Randy. He's been calling your name," said the doctor who looked like he was barely out of high school.

With sweaty palms and a lump in her throat, she asked to see him.

"Yes, I think that's what he's been waiting for," he said grimly.

"Waiting for?"

"Yes. I must warn you that he's gravely ill and won't last much longer. I think he's just been hanging on until you came."

Randy gasped. This wasn't what she expected to hear. She was supposed to be sitting with her son and his fiancée, chatting over breakfast, discussing wedding plans and their bright future. Instead, she was on her way to see her dying ex-husband who had been only a bad memory for thirty years.

She gasped when she saw him. His face was as pale as the stark-white, hospital pillowcase he was lying on. He was rail thin. His hair was grey and cut short. His face was etched with deep, craggy lines that made him look as if he were in his sixties. If she hadn't know it was Kevin, she never would have recognized him. She stared at the pitiful, shell of a man and her heart broke in two. This was the man who had once been the strong, rugged and handsome love of her life.

"Oh, Kevin," she whispered as she sat down beside him.

He struggled to open his eyes.

"Randy."

His voice was weak and barely audible.

"I'm so…so…s…sorry…"

"Sssh. Don't talk," she said as she put her finger to his lips.

She blinked back the tears that were forming.

"Le…let…let…ter…l…l…"

"Sssh. Rest, Kevin. Yes, I found the letter. I have it," she said as she took his hand. "It's all right."

"F…ff…for…give…" he said as his breath became labored.

"It's all right. It's all right, Kevin. I forgive you," she whispered.

He looked into her eyes and saw the forgiveness. It was what he was agonizing over. He didn't want to die without it. A tear rolled down his cheek as he closed his eyes for the last time. His lips were curled in a faint smile. He was finally at peace.

Randy laid her head on the bed and sobbed. There was nothing that could have prepared her for this…*any* of this. In a matter of hours, her entire life was turned inside out and upside down.

"I'm sorry, Mrs. Arnold," the young doctor said as he listened with his stethoscope and pronounced him dead.

"He was a very sick man and knew he was dying. I think he was waiting for you."

"Yes. I believe he was," Randy said tearfully.

She spent a lifetime hating and resenting the man who abandoned her and Noah. She envisioned him living a selfish, carefree life of wine, women and song, only to find he'd spiraled down into a living hell he couldn't get out of.

She never thought she would have sympathy or compassion for him and now she found herself with an unexpected emotion. Grief. And whatever was she going to do with that?

The nurse came in and handed her an envelope. In it were the few things Kevin had on him when he came into the ER. Randy reached in and pulled out an inexpensive Timex watch, a two year chip from Alcoholics Anonymous, and something completely unexpected — a silver chain, and on the chain was a wedding band. It was engraved with the initials K&R…the

one that was a match to hers...the one she put away and had long-since forgotten.

Why did he still have it and why *on earth* was he still wearing it? Why?

She was snapped back to reality when the nurse asked if she was his next of kin.

"No. Yes. Uh, I don't know," she said in a state of confusion.

The nurse looked puzzled, but she was accustomed to many different reactions from a grieving family.

"We've been divorced for thirty years and today is the first time I've seen him since then."

"Oh, I'm sorry," she said.

It was a sticky situation.

If there were no relatives or next of kin, then there was no one to take responsibility for the body and burial. In that case, he would be cremated at a local crematorium and buried in a city-run cemetery.

Randy asked what would happen if there wasn't anyone to take care of things.

The nurse explained that his ashes would be

buried in an unmarked grave with all the other unclaimed ashes.

Randy knew she couldn't let that happen. At the end of his life, Kevin sought her out to make amends and she forgave him. Despite everything, she once loved him and he *was* Noah's father.

Oh my God! Noah. He was sitting with Jen and Jack chatting over breakfast, completely unaware his father had shown up after all these years. How was she going to handle this? What was she going to tell him? *How* was she going to tell him? How do you tell your son, that the father who abandoned him and had never been in his life, was lying dead in the hospital morgue?

Randy told the nurse she would take the responsibility for his burial and left.

She stood for a moment before going into the diner, trying to decide how to handle it. Say nothing and wait until they went back to the Inn? Speak to him alone? or with Jen? She knew, that no matter what, it was going to be the most difficult conversation she would ever have with him.

She had a fleeting thought that maybe she

wouldn't tell him at all, to shield him from being hurt. It could all be done in secret and he would never have to know, but she knew, that in good conscience, she couldn't. He had a right to know.

Noah looked up and smiled when he saw her.

"Mom, I was afraid you were never coming back," he joked.

"Sorry. It was complicated."

That was the understatement of the year.

"Are you okay?" Jack asked. "You look a little rattled."

"Uh, no, I'm fine. It just took a little longer than I expected."

"So you found out who it was? Was he, or she, okay?" Noah asked.

"Yeah. I'll tell you about it later."

"Okay. We need to get you another breakfast. A hot one."

"No, that's okay. I'm not really hungry anymore."

"You should eat *something*. Maybe some toast?" Jack said.

"No, really. Just a cup of coffee."

They sat for a little while longer and then Randy told Noah it was time to go. As they got up to leave, Jack noticed that Randy's coffee cup remained untouched.

"Noah, can you go back to the Inn with me? I'd like a little alone time with you."

She tried to sound as nonchalant as possible so he wouldn't suspect anything was wrong. She was afraid her emotions were showing, as if he could visibly see her heart pounding out of her chest.

"Sure. I guess I can spare you a few minutes," he said and winked at Jen.

"That works for me, too. I'd like to spend some time with my daughter. I didn't think I'd be able to tear them apart," Jack said and chuckled.

Noah kissed Jen goodbye, unaware that a bombshell was about to explode in his lap.

Randy was silent as they drove back to the Inn. She tried calculating in her mind how she was going to start the conversation, but her mind was a complete blank.

When they got back to Randy's apartment, Noah tossed his jacket on a chair and sat down.

"Okay, Mom, what's this all about?"

Besides being exceptionally smart, Noah was also very intuitive when it came to his mother. He always knew when she had something serious on her mind.

She sat down next to him and took his hands in hers.

Uh-oh, he thought. This must be pretty bad. He searched her face and saw she was very distraught.

"It's okay, Mom. Whatever it is, it's okay."

"Noah, I just don't know how to say this."

He squeezed her hand as if to say, whatever it is, I can handle it.

She swallowed hard and began.

"Noah, this will be a big shock for you. It was for me."

His eyes widened as he leaned in a little closer.

"The man in the hospital was your father."

At first he looked puzzled and then as the

information sunk in, he stiffened.

"What?"

"Yes. Your father. He checked in here last night. Carly didn't recognize the name so she had no idea who he was. He was sitting in the dining room when we were there. I wasn't paying attention to anyone else last night and I wouldn't have recognized him anyway."

Noah didn't say anything. He waited for her to go on.

"I got the keycard from the hospital and came back to find some identification. I found his wallet and when I opened it, I couldn't believe it. It was your father's. I was totally in shock."

"Then I saw an envelope sitting on the desk and it had my name on it. I didn't know if I wanted to open it or not. I was afraid to read the letter, but I knew I had to."

Randy wasn't sure what to do next. Finish the story? Give him the letter?

As if he was reading her mind, he said, "let me see it."

She hesitated briefly, then took it out of her

purse and handed it to him.

She watched his face as he read it. Her heart went out to him. It was hard enough for *her* to read it. He was her husband, but this was Noah's *father*, the father he had never seen or heard from, the father who didn't give a crap about him. They never talked about it, but she knew Noah's anger bordered on hatred. She wanted to shield and protect him from the pain she saw in his face, but she knew she couldn't.

He laid the letter down when he finished reading it and looked at her.

"Are you okay, Mom?"

She was astounded. In the face of an intensely disturbing situation, he was worried about *her*. He was an amazing, young man.

"Yes. But how are *you*?"

He paused for a moment, thinking.

"I'm not sure, Mom. This *is* quite a shock. I don't know what to say. I'm thinking whether I should see him or not."

Randy had almost forgotten that she had even more devastating news to tell him.

He saw the expression on her face change.

"What is it, Mom?"

She paused for a moment, trying to decide how to say it.

"Noah, I'm so sorry. Your father died shortly after I got to the hospital."

Noah bowed his head and she saw tears running down his cheeks. She put her arms around him and he did the one thing she didn't expect. He started to sob.

"Oh, Noah."

Her heart was breaking. She held him tightly and felt her blouse getting wetter and wetter. She held him until he stopped crying.

"I would have liked to have seen him," he said.

"I wish there had been time to let you know about this, but as soon as he saw me, he asked for forgiveness and then passed away."

He nodded his head in sadness. He had been angry for so long at the man who abandoned him and left him fatherless. Noah never told his mother that he secretly envisioned him showing up at one of his baseball games, or chess tournaments, or his high school graduation. He secretly imagined getting a birthday card in the mail, or a Christmas present, or a letter explaining why he didn't love his son enough to stick around.

He never told his mother that he wanted his father to show up in his life because he knew how much it would hurt her. So he kept those secret longings tucked away in his heart.

And now he missed the one opportunity he had, to see the man he dreamt about his whole life.

"What happens now?" he asked.

"I have to make burial arrangements."

"I'll help you with that," he said resolutely.

She started to protest, but then she realized that Noah might *need* to be part of it, as a way of closure, a way to say goodbye.

"Okay," she said gently.

He called Jen and asked her to meet him at the Inn — he had something to tell her. And could she please bring Jack with her. This was a family matter and needed to be shared with the two people who were going to become family.

Noah and Jen spent hours talking about his father. She knew he left when Noah was a baby, but didn't know any more than that. He never talked about him and Jen never asked. She knew it was a painful subject and if he wanted her to know anything, he would tell her.

But now the floodgates were open and he shared all his emotions. She sat quietly and listened to the man she loved pour out his heart. It made her love him even more.

Jack and Randy went for a long walk and Randy shared her pain and unexpected grief. Jack talked about his wife and the grief he felt for many years after she died. They shared their deepest feelings and confidences and afterwards, Randy felt purged and at peace. When they returned to the Inn, Jack was holding her hand.

EPILOGUE

Another New Beginning

They couldn't have asked for a better day for a wedding. The sky was a clear, cerulean blue and the sun felt warm on their faces.

The bride was beautiful and the groom was nervous.

The Inn was resplendent with crystal vases filled with delicate, apricot flowers and sprays of white baby's breath. Reuben and Carly made sure the blooms were fresh and plentiful. Randy knew they could be counted on to make everything look tasteful and elegant.

Carly took great care to assure the Honeymoon Suite was as perfect as perfect could be. She had prepared the room for honeymooners before, but this was different. It had to be extra-special. When Randy checked it out, her eyes welled up. She knew that when he carried his bride across the threshold, he would be pleased. They were only going to be there for the wedding night and then they would be leaving early the next morning for their romantic honeymoon in the Caribbean.

Randy arranged for someone to cover for Carly and Reuben, as well as for Bea and Angie, so they could all attend the wedding. After all, they *were* family.

The dining room was closed for the reception. The tables, covered with white linen tablecloths and apricot napkins, were arranged in a U-shape with the center chairs reserved for the bride and groom. Large, silver candelabras and fragrant flower arrangements graced the tables.

Zach designed a lavish menu befitting the occasion. He would attend the wedding, but insisted on preparing the food himself. He simply wouldn't trust anyone else in his kitchen for such a special celebration.

There was white bunting woven through the slats of the gazebo and an abundance of flowers trailing down the trellis.

Everything was exactly the way Randy envisioned it. She wanted it to be spectacular, but it was much more than that. It was magical.

Randy put the finishing touches on her make-up, slipped on her dress and then helped Jen with hers. When they went shopping, they decided on a simple, ivory, tea-length dress — understated, yet elegant.

"Here, let me zip you," Randy said.

Jen smiled.

"Are you excited?"

"That's a silly question."

"I guess it is."

They hugged each other and laughed.

"I don't know why you're so nervous, Noah," Jack said.

"Hey, this doesn't happen every day."

"Well, *that's* for damn sure."

"Here, let me help you with that," Jack said and straightened Noah's tie.

"Thanks."

He looked at the clock and said it was time.

They headed outside to take their places in the garden, anxiously waiting for the ceremony to begin.

It was a small gathering, just the few relatives they had and their friends from the Inn. Mellow music was playing softly in the background and everyone was in their seats.

When the wedding march began to play, they rose to their feet and watched the bride walk down the aisle. She was beaming and obviously very much in love. It was the happiest day of her life.

She reached the altar and the long-awaited ceremony began.

"Who gives this woman to be married to this man?" the minister asked.

"I do," he said and stepped aside.

The minister continued.

"We are assembled here today to witness this blessed occasion. This man and this woman stand here in the presence of God to be joined in

Holy Matrimony. Let us begin."

"Do you Jack, take this woman, Randy, to be your lawfully wedded wife, to have and to hold, to love and to cherish, to honor and sustain, in sickness and in health, for richer or for poorer, and be true to her in all things until death do you part?"

Jack looked deeply into Randy's eyes.

"I do."

"Do you Randy, take this man, Jack, to be your lawfully wedded husband, to have and to hold, to love and to cherish, to honor and sustain, in sickness and in health, for richer or for poorer, and be true to him in all things until death do you part?"

With tears in her eyes, she whispered, "I do."

"May I have the rings, please?"

Noah stepped forward and handed them to the minister.

As he stepped back, he smiled at his mother.

His heart was filled with joy for the woman who raised him, loved him, unconditionally, and protected and sacrificed for him.

It was finally her turn to be happy and there was no better man to bring her that happiness than his father-in-law.

The minister handed Jack the ring intended for Randy.

"Randy, I give you this ring as a symbol of my love. Just as this circle is without end, so is my love. Just as it is unbreakable, so is my eternal commitment to you. I will love and cherish you until the end of time," Jack said as he slipped the gold band on her finger.

The minister handed Randy the other ring.

"Jack, I give you this ring that has no beginning and no end. It is a symbol of my endless love for you, as strong and precious as the gold it is made of. It is a token of my unbreakable, eternal devotion to you."

"These solemn vows are not taken lightly and signify before God that you will be steadfast in your love and commitment to each other. You have promised each other a lifetime of devotion and faithfulness 'til death do you part."

"With the power vested in me, it is an honor

to pronounce you husband and wife. You may kiss the bride."

Jack gazed into Randy's eyes with a love that was palpable and kissed her, first gently and tenderly, then passionately.

Everyone started clapping and cheering.

Jack smiled and Randy blushed.

Hand in hand, they walked back down the aisle followed by Noah and Jen.

As soon as he could, Noah threw his arms around his mother and hugged her.

"Mom, I'm so happy for you. You deserve this, and a lot more."

"Thank you," she whispered. "I don't think I've ever been so happy."

Jen hugged her dad and then Randy.

"You really *are* my Mom, now," she said.

Noah and Jen hugged each other. They were ecstatic that their parents had fallen in love and they knew they were partly responsible for bringing the two of them together. After all, if they hadn't found each other and decided to get married, their parents never would have met.

Randy and Jack had both been alone and lonely for such a long time. It was about time they found some happiness.

After the joy-filled reception, Randy and Jack retreated to the Honeymoon Suite. Many young couples had been there before, but it was different for them. They weren't youngsters. They were mature and experienced in this thing called life, and yet they were young in their love for each other.

They had so much in common. They both suffered devastating losses and hardships in their lives and spent years healing from those losses. They had both been wounded, but not broken.

Ironically, it was because of Kevin that they ultimately came together and fell in love. Jack sat for hours and let Randy pour out her heart after Kevin died. He listened to the details of Randy's marriage and divorce and of what she suffered, sheltering her son's feelings of being abandoned. She let him read Kevin's letter. It was an intimate thing that opened up their hearts to a deeper level.

They both believed it was a miracle that brought them together, not fate, but a true miracle. Randy and Jack were convinced it was their destiny.

From experience, Randy truly believed in destiny. After all, wasn't it destiny that brought Jimmy into her life when she needed him most? Wasn't it destiny that they became friends? Wasn't it destiny that when he died he gave her the gift that completely changed her life...and changed it in a way she never could have imagined.

She never imagined she would see Kevin again, forgive him and say goodbye — that she would finally have closure and be able to put the past to rest.

She never imagined Noah would be given a glimpse into his father's tortured past, and as hard as it was, be able to start healing from his own wounds. It was very hard for him, but he had Jen — his loving wife, his soul-mate — to stand by his side and walk through it with him. They were happily married, with a bright and hopeful future and expecting their first child.

But most of all, Randy never imagined

that she would someday be married to a man she loved and adored — a man who loved and adored her, too.

It was the stuff dreams were made of.

...and once again she whispered,

thank you, Jimmy...

ABOUT THE AUTHOR

Judith Sessler's love of writing began as a child. She wrote poetry on napkins and short stories in her school notebooks. Her first published works were essays and magazine articles when she was in her early twenties.

She took a writing hiatus for five years when her family moved across country and she began a career as a restaurant manager. When they moved back East, she discovered that her husband, inadvertently, discarded the box which contained everything she had ever written.

Judith was so devastated that she was unable to write another thing for twenty-five years.

Then one night, she woke up with a title stuck in her head. That was how it always happened, waking in the middle of night with a title and the next morning the story would just flow from there. The rest is history.

Judith's books run the gamut from romantic fiction, to a juvenile time-travel series, to short story collections, to this latest endeavor, a much requested sequel to FIFTY SHADES OF GREEN OR COFFEEHOUSE CONFESSIONS OF THE UNCOMMON JOE.

She continues to write every day in her "office"... Starbucks, with many thanks, as always, to her 'family' of baristas extraordinaire.

Made in the USA
Middletown, DE
04 April 2017